# Richard Diamond, USMC

a novel by
Edward F. Koehler, PhD

BookLocker.com, Inc.
2021

Second Edition

This novel is dedicated to Captain Patricia Hagan, United States Navy nurse, for her bravery and dedication to duty and country during her several tours of duty in Iraqi and Afghanistan. Captain Hagan is a wife, mother, teacher, and patriot living in New England.

I heartily thank my editor, Harry Suber, for his keen eye and constructive criticism. Mr. Suber is a schoolteacher of history and government on the eastern shore of Maryland.

I would also like to thank my wife Julie for her final read edits and constructive comments, and for her patience during the writing of Richard Diamond.

# Table of Contents

# CHAPTER 1

## The Orders

The sun emerged from behind the clouds as Richard Diamond's boots pound the ground on the Marine Corps' exercise course at Quantico, Virginia. It rained the day before, and the course was wet, the grass was wet, the trees brushing against Diamond's arms were wet. As Richard neared the end of the course, he noticed Private Thompson approaching. Lieutenant Diamond slowed up as Thompson saluted him with a casual wave of his hand against his brow. He then came to a complete stop, caught his breath, and gave a salute back.

"Lieutenant Diamond, you're wanted at headquarters ASAP."

Diamond was still breathing heavily, bent over with sweat dripping off his face. "Thanks, private " Richard huffs out as a bead of sweat hangs onto the tip of his nose. Lieutenant Diamond walked across the parking lot as he fully caught his breath. Headquarters was about a half-mile away, an easy walk on a nice spring day. Richard was elated with the possibility of seeing Major Cole's secretary Margie.

It wasn't long before Diamond was approaching the headquarters building. As he approached the front door, several other Marines were exiting. One of them held the door open for Diamond as he entered. At the reception desk was a cute blonde female Department of Defense civilian employee who recognized Lieutenant Diamond right away.

As Richard entered the office, Margie raises her head up and gives a friendly wave to Richard.

"Hello, Lieutenant Diamond! Major Cole wants to see you in his office. If you just wait a minute, I'll let them know you're here," she said looking up at Richard through her thick lashes.

Diamond waited at the desk while the young lady picked up the telephone and called Major Cole.

"Major Cole?" she paused. "Lieutenant Diamond is here to see you."

Diamond heard "Send him in" in a muffled tone come from the handheld receiver.

"Go on in Lieutenant," she said with a smile, again looking up at Richard.

Richard straightened out his running gear as best he could and knocked twice on the Major's door before entering the room. Major Cole's office was a typical USMC office. The window behind the desk was open slightly, and on the windowsill was Major Cole's pipe sitting in a cradle. Diamond had heard Major Cole was trying to quit smoking.

Major Cole was a stocky fellow with a mustache, and his hair was just starting to gray around the temples. His mustache was well trimmed, not as trimmed as William Powell of the *Thin Man*, but not as bushy as Tom Selleck in *Magnum P.I.* Major Cole and Lieutenant Diamond got along well together; they had known each other for several years and shared a mutual respect for each other's abilities. They both led their lives the cowboy way. Major Cole was dressed in camouflage fatigues, neatly pressed.

"Good morning, Major. Please excuse my appearance. I just finished the obstacle course." Diamond spoke with a slight Texas accent.

"That's okay, Diamond. This will only take a moment. First, I just received this from the Pentagon. All leaves are canceled for the foreseeable future. SECNAV has a small operation that I'd like you to take care of. The Navy has a shipment of night vision goggles and other sensitive equipment that needs to go overseas for use in an upcoming operation. I told SECNAV we could handle getting this equipment to the proper location. Would you be interested in volunteering to accompany this shipment to the desert in Iraq?"

"Yes, sir. Whatever the Marine Corps needs, I can handle. This sounds like a babysitting job for a shipment."

"Yes, Diamond, that's true. Generally I would agree with you. This could turn out to be little more than that, but I don't think so." The Major rotated in his seat, and picked up his pipe from the window sill. " We have been put on notice; be prepared to deploy within twenty-four hours. It looks like the United States is striking back at the terrorist for 911."

"Against Iran or Saudi Arabia ? "

" No, against Iraq, Sandam Husain and the Imperial Guard; we are going to finish what we should have done the last time we were there. These night vision googles and laser targeting equipment will enable Navy pilots to hit exactly what their targets are; with pin point accuracy. Like dropping a bomb down an elevator shaft of a building. The Germans took Poland in 1939 with overwhelming force, with what they called Blitzkrieg or lighting warfare. Well that battle is going to look like a school yard fight when the United States Military hits Iraqi with Shock and Awe. I hope it doesn't come to that, but if we get the call, let's be ready."

" I hope your right sir, and it gets called off. But if we have to go to war, then lets be the pointy end of the spear."

As the major spoke, Diamond was thinking. *"Should I ask the major about the promotion list? I wonder if it has come out yet. Should I ask, or should I not?* Diamond led his life the cowboy way, he was not a self- promoter, but rather let his deeds and actions speak for themselves. Finally, he spoke. "Oh, Major Cole. By the way, I was just wondering if you'd heard anything about the promotions list."

Major Cole opened up the right-hand desk drawer and removed a pouch of pipe tobacco. "No, nothing yet, Diamond, but your name is on the top of the list. You scored well on the test, and your fit reps have all been satisfactory. Hang tight. I will probably know something by the time you get back from the desert," he said, then continued. "Diamond, go on and pick up your orders from Margie. You leave in two days. You'll catch a flight out of Andrews to Germany and then take a short hop from Germany to your destination.

4

Review your orders, there is a SEAL Team that may be flying with you, they are the ones that ultimately will be using this equipment. I will see you in a few days when you get back." If Major Cole knew anything about the promotions list, he didn't let on. The Major rocked back in his chair as he filled his pipe with tobacco. The aroma of cherry and aged tobacco filled the room before Major Cole even struck the match.

"Yes, sir. Thank you, sir. See you in a few days."

Diamond left the way he came in, pulling the door closed behind him as he exited the major's office. Margie was already standing there with a large manila envelope in her hand. She handed it to Diamond as he approached. As Richard took the package, he looked perhaps a little too long at Margie. She looked as if she should be the heroine in an Alfred Hitchcock movie. She was blonde, not too tall, nice figure, with sparkling blue eyes. Today, Margie was wearing a white blouse with an open collar that exposed a strand of onyx pearls. To complement her blouse, she wore a black skirt that fell nicely around her body and stopped just above her knee. The fabric clung to her body as if it wanted to touch her. To finish her look, she wore black high heels with rounded toes and small bows.

"Oh, Richard," she said playfully. "If you're going some-place nice, bring something back for me. Nothing big. Just anything you might find nice for a girl." Her hazel blue eyes looked at Richard with the glint of a flirt.

One thing that excited Richard about Margie was her sharp wit, Richard had a penchant for smart women. "Why,

Margie, you know you're always first in my heart. I can't tell you where I'm going, but if I find anything that I think would be good for you, and I have the time, I'll pick it up," he responded in kind. " I'll see you when I get back. Maybe we can go out to dinner and a movie, again. I've been meaning to call you, but I've just been busy. So, please forgive me for not getting back to you. I had a great time with you the last time we went out." Richard finished his sentence and sensed encouragement from Margie.

"Thanks, Richard. That would be great. We did have fun together, didn't we?"

" Margie, it's short notice, but if you are not busy this weekend, let's go out to dinner. "

" That a wonderful idea Richard, I would love to see you again. "

" Good, I'll call you on Saturday, about time and other details." Richard reaches out and touches Margie's hand affectionately.

Margie was about Diamond's age, and they had gone out a couple of times before and the sexual energy between then was like static electricity, it could spark at any time. Nothing serious had happened yet, but it was only a matter of time before the hugs and kisses blossomed into something more. The memory of feeling Margie's body pressed against his, left Richard wanting for more.

Diamond took the envelope and walked past Margie back to a remote part of the office. He opened the envelope stamped in red with the word SECRET. Richard read the four-page letter carefully. *"1. Flight from Andrews to Germany........2. Flight from Germany to Iraqi, Deliver equipment. 3. Immediate return Flight back to Germany. 4. One day layover then a Flight back to Andrews. "* he thought as he read. *"By the time the real shooting starts, I'll be back at Andrews Air Force Base."*

Diamond put the letter and orders back in the envelope, resealed it with the little red string tie, and tucked it under his left arm. He walked out the door toward the parking lot where his car was parked. Richard approached his car, opened the door, tossed the envelope on the passenger seat, and slipped in behind the wheel. As Diamond turned the key in the ignition of the midnight blue, older model Corvette convertible, the 350-cubic-inch engine roared to life. He backed out of the space and took a right turn out of the parking lot heading toward his office.

Lieutenant Diamond's office was in a typical two-story, government-issue Marine Corps office building. It was a red brick building built about 50 years ago. The building looked more like a two-story college dormitory in the Georgian style, with evenly spaced double-hung windows that were painted white. It was topped by a hip roof with an attic for storage, with one window at each end.

Diamond entered and walked down the hall straight to his office. Unlocking the door, he entered and flipped the light switch on. The florescent ceiling lights flickered to life. Behind Diamond's desk was a grey four-drawer filing cabinet with the top drawer featuring a combination lock located in the center. Richard quickly turned the dial, pulled the door open, and placed the orders inside. He then carefully slid the drawer closed until the drawer gave a solid click. By habit, he then spun the lock both right and left. *"That should do it,"* he thought. Richard left his office, turning out the light, and locking the door behind him.

Back outside of the office, Richard quickly hopped back in the Vette, turned the key, and headed for the main gate. As he slowly pulled up to the main gate, the guard exited the guardhouse and gave Diamond a quick salute. Diamond slowed and saluted back as the gate rose. Diamond coasted under it, past the main gate, and out to the main road. U.S. Route 1 is the main drag through Quantico, Virginia. The guard made a notation of the time on his clipboard as Lieutenant Diamond drove away. The base security cameras capturing all the coming and going.

Diamond headed south on Route 1 toward home. The top is down and life is good. A short drive away, Diamond hit a dirt driveway on the left-hand side with unlabeled mailbox attached to an adjacent tree. Diamond pulled in and drove the quarter-mile down the pitted path of sand and gravel to his cabin. Diamond's cabin was nestled in the woods of Virginia, surrounded by large, old-growth loblolly pines and the occasional blue spruce. The cabin was a rustic two-story bungalow with the second floor featuring just a bathroom and two empty rooms; one on each side for guests. But Diamond never had any guests, at least none that stayed upstairs anyway. Out the back of the cabin and down the hill is Aquia Creek, a small tributary that emptied into the Potomac River. Aquia Creek is just deep enough to launch a sailboat.

Being a warm day and nearing noon, Diamond decided to shower outdoors. Out his master bedroom backdoor and a little to one side was an outdoor shower. Diamond stripped in his bedroom, tossed the clothes in the dirty laundry hamper, grabbed a towel from the master bathroom, and walked outside to shower. He hung the towel on a wooden peg to the side of the shower. The noonday sun added warmth to the spring fresh air.

Diamond was just over 6 feet tall, with blue eyes and sandy blonde hair that stuck up in all directions when it wasn't combed. He was in good shape, muscular, but could still stand to lose five pounds. That's why he had been running and working out on the obstacle course. People often commented that he looks a little like Robert Redford, just not as handsome.

Richard takes his shower as the midday sun beats down on him. He washes his hair with shampoo and shaves while he showers. As he does his final rinse, Richard turns the hot water off slowly so that the final rinse is cool on his body. Richard dries off standing in the sunlight, wraps the towel around his waist and reenters his bedroom through the rear door. After the shower, Diamond gets dressed in a clean set of Marine Corps fatigues and has a quick lunch of a ham and Swiss cheese sandwich on whole wheat bread with Dijon mustard. He complements the sandwich with an apple and bottled water. He grabs his keys and walks out the front door and across his sandy driveway. Back in the Corvette, he drives quickly up the driveway and makes the right-hand turn out onto Route 1. The drive back to Quantico takes less than 20 minutes.

Once through the front gate, Diamond goes directly to the firing range. He has a class of new Officer Candidate School recruits ready for pistol training. The sergeant in charge has already unlocked the gun cabinet and distributed the Colt .45 semi-automatics to the class, along with ammunition. Two .45s lie side-by-side on the table next to the sergeant.

"Good afternoon," Diamond said to the class. "Is everyone ready for day one of pistol training?" He doesn't stop for an answer. "The weapon distributed to you gentlemen is a standard-issue Colt .45 semiautomatic. It holds a clip of 11 shots. In the field, this weapon can save your life with a single, well-placed shot. The sergeant has already briefed you on loading and the general safety of this weapon."

The sergeant is a big man, well over 6 feet tall and approximately 250 pounds of solid muscle. In a booming drill sergeant voice "If everyone will take their position on the firing line, we have targets at the 50-foot distance. Please take your positions standing with the weapon holster. Starting with position one, I want you to draw your weapon, click the safety to the off position, and fire three shots at the target." His Louisiana accent evident in every syllable.

Boom! Boom! Boom!

The firing range is an outdoor facility with a covered area for participants to stand. The grass is worn down to the dirt at each location, twelve locations in all. Both Lieutenant Diamond and Gunny Sergeant Mercurio walk behind the students as they get into position.

"Good. Now shooting position number two. Same routine. Draw your weapon, go down on one knee, and fire three shots at the target."

Target practice continued for all twelve of the OCS candidates, each firing there weapon in sequence. Occasionally, either Lieutenant Diamond or the sergeant stood behind the candidate to adjust his stance, grip, or give other instructions. At the end of each shooting, the targets were retrieved and the shooter was reviewed and graded. This procedure was repeated several more times until each candidate felt comfortable with the weapon and could at least hit the target with all three single shots at 50 feet.

At the end of the class, both Sergeant Mercuio and Diamond got into the standing position, each with his .45 holstered. It took only one second for both Diamond and the sergeant to draw his weapon, click off the safety, and fire three quick shots at the target—*Boom! Boom! Boom!* The sergeant was an excellent shot; all three shots closely grouped in the middle of the target. Lieutenant Diamond was almost as good; Richard hit two good solid centers and one shot is slightly up and to the right. Richard is right-handed and when he pulled on the trigger, it tended to pull the weapon slightly to the right. As an experienced marksman, he usually holds the weapon with both hands to account for this movement as the trigger is pulled.

"Okay, gentlemen, that's enough for today. Gunny Sergeant Mercurio will be instructing the class over the next several days, and I expect good solid progress the next time I see the class. Before you all go, I want to say something about using <u>your</u> weapon in country, use it when have to, but be aware there are at least three other ways to look at any situation. Use your brain first, don't start any mission or assignment without a well thought out plan. And when the boots hit the ground, improvise, adapt, modify and overcome. " With that, Diamond dismissed the class and headed home. As Diamond walks to his car, he is passed by a group of new FBI agents, jogging in formation, heading in the opposite direction. They are all neatly dressed in blue shorts with white T-shirts with the letters "FBI" printed in dark blue. The FBI agents conduct weapons training at Quantico; Diamond's next class was scheduled with a group of new FBI recruits.

# CHAPTER 2

## The Catch

The next day was Diamond's off day. It was a Saturday, and the weather was good. It looked like a good day for fishing, so Diamond grabbed his pole, net, and other equipment and walked down the 100-yard path to Aquia Creek. Finding a good spot along the bank, he lays down under the shade of a nice, big blue spruce, cast his line in the water, and waited. A short while later, Richard gets a strike. The line began to twitch, and then with a solid hit, the rod's tip bent downward. Diamond grabbed the pole and gave it a quick jerk upward to set the hook. *Now just reel him in nice and easy and we are going to be eating fresh fish for dinner*, Richard thought. It didn't take long. Diamond was an experienced fisherman and in no time, he had a sizable brown trout laying in the grass next to him. *That should do it for today*, Diamond thought as he leisurely walked back to his cabin.

As Diamond walks up the path from the creek to his backdoor, much to his surprise, he sees Margie walking down the path toward him. He is taken back a bit since they hadn't finalized their plans for dinner that evening.

"Well, good afternoon," says Diamond. Smiling he approaches Margie and gently kisses her lips. Margie is dressed in white canvas sneakers, with white ankle socks. She wears a pair of khaki Bermuda shorts and a white boat neck tee shirt with colorful stripes, she looks fabulous.

"This is definitely an unexpected surprise," Says Richard in an exaggerated Texas drawl.

"I know we were going to have dinner tonight Richard but since you're going away, I thought we should spend a little time together this afternoon….have dinner later….and just be together before you need to go," responds Margie with a smile. With that Richard and Margie slowly walk back up to the cabin. As they approach the back door, Richard opens the door for Margie and says, " how about I clean this beautiful trout I've just caught, I'll fix some lunch for us and then let's go for a walk back down to the creek. We'll make it a picnic. It is one of my favorite places to go and I'd really enjoy being there with you. "

As Richard and Margie enter the kitchen, he places the fish in the sink, takes some ice out of the refrigerator, and places it on top of the fish. Richard then washes his hands, smiles and says, "since this is your first visit here, how about I give you a tour of my humble home before I finish cleaning the fish and we go for our picnic and walk?"

"That sounds good to me" replies Margie.

The tour is brief since the cabin is simple and rustic. It is not cluttered in the least, in fact it is neat and tidy as they walk around the living room. The thick outside stone walls show through to the inside walls and the most outstanding item is the large stone fireplace. It is large enough to allow a small woman of Margie's size to fit inside of it. The furnishings are masculine with a soft brown leather sofa, a matching chair and mahogany tables with brass lamps atop the tables. There are magazines on a matching coffee table and a few paintings on the walls. The paintings are varied in style and a framed photograph of Richard with the commandant of the Marine Corpse sits on the fireplace mantle.

Richard walks through to the master bedroom to finish the tour of the downstairs as Margie follows. Being in this room together excites Richard and as he glances at Margie, she appears to be feeling the same way. Suddenly anticipation of being with each other for the first time overwhelms Richard as he looks down at Margie and gently takes her hand. He pulls her toward him and presses his body up against her. He kisses her warmly and affectionately and she responds as their bodies move closer and closer.

As Richard and Margie cross the room, he moves Margie toward the bed. They kiss again as they stand just by the bed and Richard then removes Margie's Tee shirt revealing her breasts and small pink nipples. They kiss again and Richard slowly pulls down Margie's shorts and panties. He then removes his clothes one piece at a time with Margie just looking at him as he does this. Shoes are quickly askew on the floor, his tee shirt and finally his pants and olive drab boxer shorts. They sit on the side of the bed and then Margie rolls over and is laying on the bed face down, her round, bare bottom showing no tan lines.

Richard kneels on the bed and leans forward. He starts kissing Margie on her bottom and then slowly begins to work his way up her back; he plants soft kisses all the way to the

15

nape of her neck. When Richard reaches Margie's neck, she rolls over and embraces him, pulling him down on top of her. Margie's pulse quickens, her breathing hastens, and she begins to feel slightly faint. Richard wraps his muscular arms around her. They both extend themselves with their bodies fully touching. Richard shifts positions slightly, kissing Margie on her neck and working his way down the front of her body, kiss by kiss. He places his right hand between Margie's legs and slowly strokes her as he continues down her body with small nibbles and kisses. Margie is a natural blonde, with a closely trimmed pubic bush in the shape of a heart. As Richard reaches the center of Margie's blonde heart, he places his right hand beneath her bottom and his left hand on her lower abdomen. Wisps of blond hair tickle Richard's nose as he breaths in the exiting mix Margie's natural aroma and body wash.

Margie's scent fills Richard's nostrils, making them tingle. Richard adores the warmth and closeness of Margie; the heat between them is palpable. It doesn't take long for Margie to respond favorably by clenching her rear and raising her pelvis up to meet Richard's kisses and licks. Margie is thrusting her pelvis upward with greater and greater enthusiasm. Then, with one or two strong thrusts upward, she collapses backward, again lying flat on the bed. Her breathing is short and erratic as she pulses with pleasure.

Richard lies on top of Margie, both of their bodies extended fully as Richard and Margie kiss. Margie can taste her own sweet juices on Richard's lips and tongue.

"Well, Richard, you really know how to please a girl," she purrs. "That was absolutely wonderful." Her voice is soft, warm, and inviting all at the same time. Margie wraps her legs around Richard as Richard moves inside her. Richard begins to move up and down, in and out. Margie is wet and warm, a wonderful feeling as she surrounds Richard. Richard makes love to Margie slowly, as they move closer and closer together. Margie lies back and gives in to Richard completely, wrapping her arms around him, pulling him deep inside her. In a short while, Margie begins to pulsate, exciting Richard beyond the point of restraint. As Richard quickens his pace, he explodes with pleasure.

Margie and Richard spend the next two hours making love and lounging in bed listening to classical music and eventually taking a much-needed nap. Margie lies tucked in Richard's muscular arms as they drift off to sleep.

Richard wakes up first and gets up, leaving Margie to sleep in his bed under the sheet as he quietly goes into the kitchen. Richard glances back to see the bed sheet clings to every curve of Margie's body, as if it wants to linger longer, touching her. Richard pulls on his olive drab boxer shorts, khakis, and tee shirt as he reaches the kitchen. He removes the fish from beneath the remaining ice and fillets the fish into two nicely portioned pieces. He places the fillets on aluminum foil, covers them with sliced oranges, sliced Vandalia onions, half a cup of orange juice, salt, pepper, and other seasonings and places the packet in the oven.

Diamond thinks, *"Well, what do I have in the house that will go perfectly with fish fillet?* He peers into his refrigerator, but nothing's there. *Well it'll have to be fish and rice. Very simple but very nutritious. Dark chocolate Ghirardelli squares for desert.*

Margie awakens just as the broiled fish and oranges are finishing and the rice in the rice cooker is steaming. The aroma of roasted oranges fills the cabin.

Margie stirs awake and rolls over under the sheets in Richard's bed. The room smells of sex. Margie slides under the sheets to one side and sits up. The sheet falls behind Margie as she sits up, exposing her naked body to the sunlight streaming through the windows. She takes a deep breath and stretches her arms. Margie stands up and walks across the room to the master bath.

Margie's bare feet make a soft padding sound on the uneven old forest pine wood floor as she crosses the room. She steps into the shower and washes off using Richard's Irish Spring soap.

Richard crosses back through the master bedroom and enters the master bathroom. He sees Margie about the step out of the shower and holds out a large, white terrycloth towel. He hands the towel to Margie, which she takes and starts to dry her arms and legs. Richard gives Margie a little kiss, then exits the bedroom, crosses the living room past the large stone fireplace.

Margie looks in the mirror and thinks, *I have sex hair, where is Richard's brush?* Margie looks around and finds a hair brush. She runs the brush through her hair, thinking as she looks in the mirror, *That's not too bad. It will have to do.* Hanging on the back of the master bathroom door is a large fluffy white terrycloth robe. The robe surrounds Margie, she pulls the white waistband and ties it in half a bow. Margie exits the bathroom and quietly walks across the bedroom toward the door. Richard's bedroom smells of making love. Margie breathes in the aroma deeply.

Just as Margie is about to leave the bedroom, she pauses by a built-in bookcase next to the bedroom door. The top shelf is filled with books detailing engineering, thermodynamics, chemistry, and physics. The next shelf down is filled with military books, strategies, and big battles. The final shelf is stocked with mysteries, with authors such as Alfred Hitchcock, Sue Grafton, Ellery Queen, and Dashiell Hammett. Two books are not stacked up with the others but are laying on top of the mysteries, *A Brief History of Time* by Stephen Hawking and Aldous Huxley's *Brave New World*.

From the bedroom comes Margie's sweet voice, "Richard, I was just looking over your bookcase. You have a very wide selection of literature. What are you reading right now?"

"I'm halfway through Stephen Hawking's *A Brief History of Time*. I'm trying to learn the origins of the universe, the Big Bang theory, and gravitational effects on particles and waves," comes the reply from the kitchen.

19

"What about Aldous Huxley?"

"That was a gift. It's next on my list to read."

Margie walks through the bedroom door and gazes across the living room, past the large stone fireplace at Richard making dinner in the kitchen. "Can I help you?" she says sweetly.

"Sure! You could set two places at the table. Dinner will be ready in about two minutes. Would you care for wine? I think I have a cold Chardonnay in the little refrigerator over there." Richard points to a small wine frig with a glass door mounted under the kitchen counter.

Margie emerges from the bedroom in the white robe and bare feet. She walks over to a small refrigerator tucked under the counter and opens the glass door. She selects a Barefoot Chardonnay. "Is Barefoot okay?" she asks inquisitively.

"The Barefoot is fine; how appropriate I might add. Here, let me open that. Glasses are in the cabinet by you, on the first shelf," Richard says dryly as he motions toward the cabinets.

Margie opens the nearby cabinet and selects two wine glasses. Richard opens the wine and pours two generous glasses. "These are beautiful glasses Richard. Are they antique?"

"Yes, in fact, they are. I picked those up at a yard sale in my hometown of Lubbock, Texas. An elderly couple that lived around the block passed away. Their children had a yard sale to get rid of all their parent's belongings. They had these glasses and the others you see up in the cabinet priced for sale individually. I thought it was such a shame to break up the beautiful set, so I bought all of them. The older couple was married in 1922, and I believe this was one of their wedding presents. Mr. and Mrs. Holly."

Both Margie and Richard raise their glasses. Richard toasts, "Although we missed our picnic, to a wonderful afternoon."

"Thank you, Margie, you were wonderful."

"You were wonderful, Richard. Absolutely great." Margie says, blushing. Her cheek turn red as she smiles with memories of only an hour or so.

Margie and Richard enjoy a candlelit dinner of fish, rice, and wine. Dinner conversation turns from books to childhood memories; experiences that shape who you are.

" Richard, tell me about your childhood, what was it like? "

" I had the usual childhood, I had a paper route for my hometown local paper, I cut grass for extra spending money, and went swimming and fishing in the local river."

" Tell me more Richard, what is your fondest childhood memory ? "

" Oh I don't know what to say. My childhood was happy. We didn't have a lot of money.  My mother died when I was a toddler, and my father was in the Navy, so my sister and I went to live with my grandmother."

" I'm so sorry Richard, I didn't mean to pry. "

" Don't be sorry, the past is in the past. My father although career Navy was home often and his influence on me is much of who I am today.   My grandmother was both loving and stern, giving out wooden spoon discipline at the same time. "

" What is wooden spoon discipline"

" Well if you got out of line, she would hit you with a wooden spoon."

"That's terrible!"

" Well, I didn't like it at the time, but now I love it, really. Okay, here's an example of why I love my childhood and why it has shaped me into who I am.  We were poor, I just didn't know it when I was a kid. When I was about seven or eight years old, my grandmother would send my over to our family doctors, Doc Mounts. He had the biggest house in town, and in his front yard was the biggest apple tree you have ever seen. So, my grandmother would send me over there with a bushel basket in my red wagon to get apples. Just get the ones that are on the ground, don't climb the tree, she would say. So, over I would go, red wagon in tow, and return with all the apples that would fit in the basket and in the wagon."

"What a nice story, go on. "

"My grandmother would then make apple pies. There would be apple pies on every counter in the kitchen. Apple pies were made with cinnamon and natural unbleached sugar. The whole house would smell of baked apples and cinnamon for two days. Then she would send me back over to Doc Mounts house with pies in the red wagon. I think she was paying off our doctor bills with pies, but I'm not sure about that. At the time I thought she was just making apple pies, but now I know she was making better grandchildren."

"That is such a nice story, Richard. "

"I also learned how to bake apple pies, so if you are in need of a pie for an occasion, I'm your guy."

After dinner, Margie gets dressed and she and Richard sit on some large Redwood Adirondack chairs on the front porch eating Ghirardelli dark chocolate squares for desert.

"Margie," Richard begins softly. "I would love to have you stay over tonight, but I have to get up early and drive to DC. Perhaps we can do it another time when I get back," Richard musters all the tenderness he can put into words.

As the sun begins to sink below the horizon, and the evening cools off a little, Richard kisses Margie goodbye as she walks to her car. Margie turns and waves goodbye and he waves back. "See you when you get back in a few days!" Margie says. Margie drives a black Mercedes-Benz, two-door coupe. An expensive car for a government secretary. Richard has always assumed that Margie has money from sources other than her work. On the back windshield is a Princeton University parking sticker.

As Margie drives off, Richard walks back into the house and returns to his bedroom. He breaths in the air and smiles, thinking to himself, *"The room smells like Margie."*

# CHAPTER 3

# The Atlantic Flight

The next morning, Richard wakes early to the buzzing sound of his alarm clock. He dresses in standard Marine Corps-issue camouflage fatigues. As Richard finishes getting dressed, he picks up his cell phone off the dresser, places it in his front pocket, and buttons the button. He then puts on the only expensive item of jewelry he owns, a TAGHeuer watch. Richard consumes a breakfast of granola with 2% milk and raisins. He has a mug of coffee with milk and unprocessed raw sugar. Richard exits his front door and reaches into his pocket to retrieve his keys. There are only three keys on Richard's key ring: his house key, the key to the Corvette, and his office door key.

Richard walks across his sand driveway and slides in behind the wheel of the Corvette. Richard drives out his driveway and makes a right-hand turn onto Route 1 to Quantico. It is early in the morning and traffic is light. The dark blue Corvette roars to every touch of Richard's foot. Upon arriving at the base, Richard is waved in past the guard shack and goes straight to his office to retrieve his orders.

He enters the building and walks down the dimly lit hall. There appears to be no one else in the building. Richard opens his office door and switches on the light. He turns the dial on his combination lock and opens the top drawer of his file cabinet. The orders are right where Richard left them. Picking them up, he tucks them under his arm. Richard locks the file cabinet drawer and gives the dial a spin. With the orders in hand, Richard exits his office, locks his office door retraces his steps down the dim hallway. Richard exits his building and crosses the parking lot.

Back in his beloved Corvette, he exits the main gate, and turns right on Route 1. It is only about a mile drive to the exit that leads to I-95 North to Washington DC. Diamond merges onto I-95 and shifting through the gears, cranks the Corvette up to a cruising 75 mph. An hour and 20 minutes later, he's at the front gate of Andrews Air Force Base in the Maryland suburbs of Washington DC. Diamond pulls up to the front gate and shows his military ID; he is waved through with some basic instructions of where to go, and given a cardboard placard to place on his dash. " Here Lieutenant, please fill this card out, and then leave it on your dash when you park. " Diamond follows the airman's directions to main hangar 2B. Parking his car alongside what appears to be other civilian cars, Richard puts the top up, locks the car, and enters through the side door of hangar 2B where he is met by an airman with clipboard in hand.

"Morning Lieutenant….Are you Lieutenant Diamond?" The airman asks nonchalantly.

"Yes, airman that's me. Here are my orders." Diamond responds with the same level of casualness. The airman opens the orders, looks at them and hands them back to Diamond.

"Right this way, sir. Your package is on this pallet right here."

Sitting in the corner of the hanger is a pallet with a large cardboard box approximately 4 ft. x 4 ft. x 4 ft. wrapped with waterproof shrink wrapping and a parachute top. Just as Diamond walks over to the package, a red light above starts flashing, and the main hanger doors start to open. Outside is a Lockheed C-130 Hercules transport, with its turboprop engines just warming up. The rear load bay is down and some airman are loading items into the transport with forklifts.

"Your ride will be ready to go in about 90 minutes, Lieutenant. If you want to use the facilities or get a cup of coffee, now's the time," says the airman.

"No, thank you. I had a cup at home this morning. I'm good," Diamond said in return.

"Okay, then, Lieutenant. Just sign here, and the package is all yours." The airman hands a clipboard to Richard. Lieutenant Diamond signs the document at the bottom and hands the clipboard back to the airman. The airman tears off one sheet from the bottom, hands it back to Diamond, and says, "We're good, Lieutenant, the package is all yours." The Airman then waves to a forklift sitting in the hanger doorway, which is waiting for the signal to load up.

The next thing Diamond watches is the forklift pulling up to the package, picking it up, and loading it inside the C-130 transport in no time. Diamond walks on board, finds one of the many seats along the side, straps himself in, puts on the ear phones, and readies himself for a nap. *There's nothing to do.* He thinks. *The pilots have everything under control. All I have to do is watch a package.* Diamond is now sitting inside the C-130 with his arms folded across his chest and his head down. *Maybe I can sleep through the flight.* Richard thinks as he drifts off to sleep. *This is starting out to be the easiest assignment I've ever had.*

Richard is awakened by the noise of the rear door closing. The pilot, copilot, and navigator stroll past Richard and up to the front of the plane. The pilot turns back and walks over to Richard.

"You must be Diamond," he starts. "You're our only passenger. Sorry, there's no flight attendants and no movie. We have some magazines up front if you get bored." With that the pilot turns and heads toward the cockpit.

The C-130 taxies out, and the engines begin to whine louder and louder. The big plane starts to move down the runway, now faster, a little bumpy. Then they are airborne, nice and smooth. *Only seven or eight more hours and we will be in Germany.* Richard settles in for the long flight.

The flight over the Atlantic is uneventful. Richard strolls around the interior of the big airplane, occasionally looking at the other boxed equipment strapped down in the central bay. Out the window Richard can only see the deep blue Atlantic for as far as the eye can see in both directions. For lunch Richard eats two granola bars, and a couple of hard boiled eggs and drinks a bottle of water that he brought along. The hours drag on endlessly as the big airplane lumbers across the Atlantic. Richard returns to his seated nap position.

*Approximately 8 hours later...*

The hydraulic whine of wheels coming down and flaps being placed into position awakens Diamond. He looks out the window and sees they are over Germany and approaching Ramstein Air Force Base. It only takes a single approach, and the big C-130 lands with the wheels screeching painfully and a puff of blue smoke appearing. In no time, the C-130 is taxiing toward an open hangar. The plane comes to a complete halt, and the pilot, copilot, and navigator appear from the cockpit. All three airman walk toward Diamond and the controls to open the rear loading hatch. With the pull of a few switches, the loading hatch lowers and other government personnel start to enter and examine the cargo. Diamond walks down the ramp and is immediately met by a U.S. Air Force captain.

"You must be Lieutenant Diamond," the captain starts. "We've been expecting you. Follow me, and I'll show you the mess and where you can get cleaned up. Lieutenant, we have about a three-hour layover while we refuel and offload most of this other cargo. We'll then get you a new crew for your destination. Lieutenant, let me introduce you to Navy SEAL Team One. They will be accompanying you and the cargo to its final destination."

Across the hanger are four Navy SEALs, sitting, slouching, sleeping and eating on a well used sofa and easy chair that sit adjacent to a row of tall lockers.

SEAL Team One is a four-man team, headed by Sergeant J. Willard Whyte, who is supported by Corporal Leroy Jethro Gibbs, Corporal Zack Miller, and Seaman Second-class Charlie Mack Blackstone. Corporals Gibbs and Miller stand back as Sergeant Whyte approaches.

The airman says, "Lieutenant Diamond, this is Sergeant J. Willard Whyte, J W for short. He's the leader of SEAL Team One."

Sergeant Whyte steps forward and extends his hand to Lieutenant Diamond," nice to meet you, Lieutenant. Thanks for the equipment you're bringing us. It looks like we are going to need it in the next few days," the sergeant says contritely.

"Thank you, Sergeant. My orders are to see that this package gets delivered to a landing strip in the middle of the desert. If you know something other than this, now would be a good time to share it."

"No, sir. That's the same orders we have, and you can call me J W, everybody does. We will be going with you and hopping off with the package for distribution. It's my understanding that the package contains the newest night vision goggles and four new laser targeting compliments, along with four GPS laptop targeting units that sync with the lasers. We will be met on the ground by local militia that will serve as guides and set us up in an observation post."

The other Navy SEALs have risen and are now walking over to meet Richard.

J W gives the introductions, " this is Big Mack, he's our communications and language specialist for this mission. He speaks Farsi, Arabic and Hindi, and never met a hamburger he didn't like. The two lackluster snake eaters behind Big Mack are the Law Firm of Gibbs and Miller. If anybody gets out of line, Gibbs and Miller will lay down the law to them."

"Okay then, Sergeant. I'm going to grab something to eat in the mess, and I'll meet you back here in an hour." With that, Diamond turns and walks toward the adjoining building with a big blue arrow on it indicating "MESS."

As Richard is walking away, he can hear J W telling the men to " get your gear squared away, check your ammo, and prepare for departure."

# CHAPTER 4

# The Mediterranean Flight

S EAL Team One continues checking their personal gear, backpacks, and weaponry. Sergeant Whyte is an average looking younger Marine Corps sergeant. He has short-cropped hair and is of medium complexion. Corporal Gibbs is the tallest of the Marines at about 5 ft. 11 inches tall. Gibbs has light-brown hair and carries the sharpshooter's rifle slung over his shoulder. At approximately 24 years old, Gibbs is in the best physical shape of his life. He is a lean 180 pounds of solid muscle. Gibbs is a native of West Virginia, and it is said he can shoot at Jack rabbit in mid-hop at 100 yards with a .22 caliber rifle. Zack Miller is the youngest of them all and serves as the communications/ radio man for the group. Miller has red hair with a fair complexion and is clearly of Irish or Scottish descent. Charlie Big Mack Blackstone is a large African-American man from somewhere in the South, based on his accent. Blackstone seems almost disinterested in what everyone else is doing and instead is concentrating on finishing the rest of a cheeseburger and milkshake. Blackstone is the language translator with the team.

Three hours have passed, and it is now getting late in the evening. With the sun starting to set in Germany, the C-130 is just turning over its engines, and the ground crew and copilot are finishing their final inspection.

The copilot and Lieutenant Diamond walk up the rear ramp together and Lieutenant Diamond takes a seat across from the four Navy SEALs who are already on board. A few minutes later, the pilot and copilot come back from the cockpit and ask to speak with Diamond and Whyte.

"Okay, here's how this is going to work. As we get over the Mediterranean, we're going to turn on a false signal. Any ground radar that picks up this plane should get a response indicating we're a Russian passenger jet on a normal flight to Baghdad. This should get us past Libya, Syria, and Egypt. When we get near the Iraqi border, we're going to go down low and hopefully fly under all the radar.  By this time, it will be the middle of the night. We're hoping to hit the landing strip in the middle of the desert in pitch black around midnight. If all goes well, we land, we are on the ground no more than five minutes, the package gets delivered.  We turn and take off and fly back to Italy, easy peasy lemon squeezy."

With that short conversation, the pilot and copilot returned to the cockpit, cranked up the engines, and taxied onto the runway. The C-130 turboprop engines roar to life, and the Hercules is ready to take off into the darkness. The Hercules taxis to the far end of the runway and makes a turnaround heading south. The engines come to full force as the big plane rumbles down the runway. Richard looks across the cargo bay at the four Navy SEALs. He looks over the four young men, each with his own special skill, who are in top physical condition and mentally sharp. Richard thinks, *I'll be glad when I can get this package on the ground and head for home. It has been a long day, and now there's a long night ahead. Then it will be over, just like the pilot said. Easy peasy lemon squeezy.*

The next few hours went smoothly, just as if they were a Russian commercial passenger jet flying over the Mediterranean heading south and then southeast. Then, with no word from the cockpit, everyone felt the plane descending. Diamond's ears pop from the change in altitude, and he figured they were closing in on the drop point. The heat from the desert floor was now so hot it started to affect the plane's interior. The landing gear hydraulics began to whine as the landing gear drops, and then the flaps move into their landing position.

Without warning they come under ground fire, machine gun fire—Bam…Bam…Bam—rifling through the fuselage. The smell of jet fuel fills the plane as the pilot accelerates to gain altitude and escape the gun fire. The pilot makes a fast and tight left turn as the plane takes on more gunfire from below. Bullets tear through the fuselage. We hear rocket-propelled grenades launching outside, but they all miss. They did not take a direct hit, but shrapnel showers the plane.

*In the cockpit*

Small arms fire starts hitting the big C-130 from the ground. Both the pilot and the copilot do their best to maneuver the lumbering aircraft up and out of danger.

They pull back hard on the yolks, turn hard as they accelerate. An alarm sounds— beep…beep…beep. The copilot scrambles, "We have radar that's locked on us."

Coolly and calmly, the pilot says, "I got it. Prepare to release countermeasures."

"Captain, radar detects missile just fired. We have about ten seconds," the copilot warns.

"Hold on those countermeasures. Just keep climbing," comes the reply.

"Five seconds to impact!"

"Release countermeasures. Hard right turn."

"Countermeasures away. Come on…pick them up," says the copilot.

Then there's an explosion. The countermeasures worked. More alarms go off in the cockpit; the instrument panel is a Christmas tree of blinking red lights.

"Captain, we have taken at least three hits. It looks like left-side landing gear hydraulics and the reserve fuel tank is losing pressure."

"Turn on the fuel transfer pump. See if we can transfer the reserve tank fuel into the main tank. I'll be right back. I'm going to go back and check on damages in cargo."

*In the cargo bay*

"Is everyone all right?" calls out Sergeant Whyte.

"Over here, sergeant. I've been hit," one of the Navy SEALs answers. Seaman Blackstone is hit in the right hip. He's bleeding and losing consciousness. The Navy SEALs spring into action. Corporal Gibbs opens the medical kit and takes out a pair of scissors. He cuts away Seaman Blackstone's uniform and applies a premade, packaged dressing. Gibbs and Miller then tape it down tight to restrict the blood flow. Corporal Miller pulls out a prefilled hypodermic needle and injects the wounded man in the leg.

"It looks like you're going to sit this one out, Blackstone," says Sergeant Whyte.

The pilot comes out of the cockpit and approaches. "Is everyone okay back here?"

"No," answers Whyte. "I have a man who's hit and needs medical attention."

"Okay. Here's what we're going to do. We're going to make a pass at the alternate drop site about 30 miles from here. Everyone and all equipment goes out at 2500 feet. We are losing fuel and have lost some hydraulics. When everyone is away, we're going to turn and try to make it back to Italy."

Sergeant Whyte looks directly at Lieutenant Diamond. "Are you coming with us or are you going back with the plane?"

"My orders are to see that this equipment gets on the ground and into the hands that need it. So, I guess that means I jump with you guys."

Turning their attention to the pilot, Whyte says, "Captain, where are your parachutes?"

"In this locker," the pilot says as he opens a locker in the cargo bay. "US Airforce steerable jump chutes. Good up to 250 pounds."

Sergeant Whyte again looks directly at Richard, "Okay, then, get the body armor off of Blackstone." Turning to the team, he says, "SEAL team, get a parachute on and strap yourself in. We've got about three minutes before we jump." Turning again to Diamond, he orders, "Here, take this rifle. You may need more than your side arm." The Navy SEALs quickly pull on the parachutes, moving their packs to the front.

As quickly and as efficiently as they could, everyone takes the body armor off of the wounded Seaman Blackstone. Diamond puts on the body armor and parachute and pulls the straps tight.

"Are you an experienced jumper," asks Sergeant Whyte.

"Yes, I have about 20 jumps under me, along with about 10 skydives from 12,000 feet."

With that the rear door starts to open on the C-130 transport. A swirl of wind blows through the cargo bay. The men pull their goggles down and, looking around at each other, they all give the thumbs up.

"Okay, everyone, we are attaching a tether to the package. It goes out, and the shoot opens automatically," yelled Whyte over the engine noise and wind. "We all go out right after it. Meet on the ground at the package. See you all in a few minutes."

The steady red light above the rear door turns from red to solid green. With that, the three Navy SEALs and Diamond push the package out the back of the giant Hercules, and the tether line pulls tight and opens the shoot. The tether flaps helplessly in the wind out the back of the giant plane.

Sergeant Whyte and his SEAL team walk to the edge of the cargo bay in unison, like they had rehearsed the choreography. The sergeant holds up his left hand with five fingers boldly displayed, then four, three, two, one, and the three SEALs are out the door. Richard stands there looking out the door as he walks to the edge of the cargo bay …

*Oh, what have I gotten myself into this time?* he thinks as he jumps. With a short step, Richard is out the back of the plane and in the W position. Diamond coasts through the skies for a mere five seconds before he sees the parachutes of the Navy SEALs open below him. He pulls his rip cord, and his parachute deploys. The sudden jerk of the deceleration snaps his head back and jolts his entire body.

Richard grabs the top toggle lines for steering and follows the other parachutes toward the ground. Diamond hits the desert sand just as he pulls on the toggle lines. He makes a short roll and is up on his feet, pulling the parachute toward him. Richard rolls up the chute and tucks the olive drab silk under his arm. He and the three Navy SEALs have landed in the desert, all within about 50 yards of each other. Even in the desert night, they can see each other clearly.

Within three or four minutes, all three Navy SEALs and Lieutenant Diamond are on the ground, chutes rolled up and standing by the package. Sergeant Whyte pulls out a satellite phone from Corporal Miller's backpack, while Corporal Miller pulls out a collapsible satellite dish. Miller unfolds the dish like a small aluminum umbrella. Holding the dish in his right hand and looking at his compass on his left wrist, Miller points the dish toward the southern sky. With a few presses of the buttons, Sergeant Whyte connects with Navy communications somewhere either in the Mediterranean or in the Indian Ocean. He advises them that one team member is wounded, that they have provided him with first aid, and he is on the plane back to Sigonella Air Station, Sicily. He also advises them that Lieutenant Diamond is with them.

"Lieutenant, Navy command says we are to read you into this operation fully. You are now in charge. This SEAL Team One and another SEAL team we will meet on the ground, will be the forward targeting spotters for an air operation that starts in one or two days depending on the weather and political factors."

They quickly cut away the shrink wrap and take out the equipment; everyone loads up with backpacks, and Sergeant Whyte pulls out his map, flashlight, and a compass. All four men are loaded with heavy packs. In addition, they are carrying two other packs between them using arm straps. Everyone is dressed in desert camouflage.

"It looks like we're about six or seven clicks that way from the outskirts of Baghdad. The sun will be up in about an hour and a half. Let's get going." Sergeant Whyte points across the desert clearly indicating the direction the men are to start walking. The men set out across the desert two by two. Sergeant Whyte and Lieutenant Diamond are out in front with one of the extra backpacks between them, Corporal Gibbs and Miller are following behind with another extra backpack between them. The desert wind begins to pick up.

# CHAPTER 5

# The Hideaway

The sun rises as SEAL Team One approaches the outskirts of Baghdad. The men are sweating, goggles on, as the hot desert sun and stiff winds hit them with sand from all directions. The temperature is now approximately 100°F, but the sun is barely up.

The outskirts of Baghdad are dotted with several industrial areas, and the SEAL team approaches one of those industrial complexes. As the men work their way down what appears to be a deserted alley, in a run-down and banal part of town. They come to an opening between the buildings and about half a block away is a large warehouse, devoid of freshness. The warehouse is well lit, including the parking lot. From their vantage point, they see the truck bay doors are open, and about 30 men are busily loading boxes into trucks with canvas tops and side covers. The boxes are nondescript wooden boxes approximately 2 ft. x 2 ft. x 3 ft. tall. The top of each box is painted in several different colors. Some box tops are painted red, others are painted yellow and others painted blue and green. The trucks into which the boxes are being loaded are Iraqi army trucks, with armed guards on all sides. Other trucks are parked on the street facing the warehouse, but close to SEAL Team One. The large warehouse doors are all in the open position. J W and Richard peer through binoculars to get a closer look, inside the warehouse and at the wooden boxed cargo.

Diamond and the Navy SEALs stay hidden behind a garage. "Diamond, what do you make of this?" asks Sergeant Whyte.

"It looks like the Iraqi army is moving some sort of weaponized material, either heavy armory shells or even be chemical or biological weapons. At the pace they're going, the warehouse looks like it's going to be empty in one or two days. Let's make a note of the location, pass the information on to the Naval Command Center, and see if they can get a satellite to track the truck movements. Other than that, we'll just pass them by."

"We have no way of tracking them anyway," says Sergeant Whyte.

"Just a moment Sergeant. If I can get close enough to one of the trucks, I can hide my cell phone on the truck somewhere," says Richard as he extracts his personal cell phone from his front vest pocket.

"What are you doing carrying a cell phone with you?"

"Well, truth be told, I didn't expect to be on the ground here. I expected to be in Germany right now sitting in a bar somewhere drinking at Tanqueray and tonic." With that Richard Diamond starts to creep down the alley closer and closer to some of the parked trucks near the front entrance. Richard approaches the truck closest to him and farthest from the building. The driver seems absent. Richard approaches the truck as stealthily as he can, turns his cell phone on, but does not press any numbers. Richard approaches from the passenger side, opens the door as quietly as he can. As soon as he gets the door open, he sees the truck driver lying down on the seat asleep. The driver awakens with a stir and sleepily speaks in his native language.

As soon as the truck driver realizes Richard is a foreigner—and a member of a foreign army—he jumps into action, knocking Richard to the ground. Richard flips the truck driver over his head with one quick move. The truck driver, now on his back and slightly out of breath, takes hard punches in the head from Richard. He knocks the driver's head backward against the pavement. In just three quick punches, the driver is knocked out. Richard rises and looks around to see if anyone has noticed the commotion.

Up the alley 200 feet away, all three Navy SEALs have their weapons trained on the guards at the warehouse. The warehouse guards apparently haven't heard anything, and do not recognize any danger. The guards continue to mill around talking and smoking. Richard places his cell phone under the passenger seat, tucking it in as deep as he can reach. He shuts the door quietly. The driver is a relatively small man, skinny, weighing no more than 150 pounds. Richard grabs him by one arm and pulls him into a sitting position. Holding onto the arm, Richard squats and lifts the driver onto his shoulder. With the driver on his shoulders, Richard trudges back up the alley where the Navy SEALs are hidden.

"Okay. Now what do we do? We can't take him with us, and we can't let him wake up, that's for sure," says Richard as he returns. "He's just a civilian driver; he's not wearing a uniform. He's just a hired driver who doesn't know any better."

Sergeant Whyte speaks up, "Look, let's just tie him up, and hide him somewhere, maybe in the trunk of a car. By the time he's found, we will be miles from here."

"Okay. Gag him, tie his hands and feet. Corporal Gibbs, in your medic kit do you have something that will knock this guy out?" Richard says as Corporal Miller pulls several large black cable ties from his backpack. Corporal Miller ties the unconscious driver's hands behind his back and ties his ankles together.

"Yes, Sir. I can knock him out for at least 12 hours," says the corporal as he hunches off his knapsack and begins to pull out the medical kit.

"Okay, then, that's our plan. We knock him out and find a car or some other place to hide him."

The SEALs start to scavenge around the alley looking into every garage they can safely get a look into. "In here Lieutenant! I think we found what we're looking for," says Gibbs.

Gibbs pull a hypodermic needle from his medical kit and with the precision of an operating room nurse, injects the driver in the arm.

Richard and Whyte join the corporal at a garage housing an older Pontiac. The Pontiac is dusty, doesn't look like it's been moved for several years. The tires are flat.

"Perfect. Put him in the trunk, and let's be on our way. Sergeant Whyte, call this in to SECNAV, and let's get out of here," says Richard as he turns to the other SEALs. "Check his pockets to see if there's anything we can use."

The keys to the Pontiac are not in the ignition, but Richard pulls on the sun visor, a set of keys drops into his hands. Richard tosses the keys to Gibbs. "Here. Lock him in the trunk."

Gibbs and Miller carry the truck driver by his arms and legs to the rear of the old Pontiac. While Gibbs opens the trunk, Miller goes through the truck driver's pockets, but finds nothing. With the truck driver's pockets turned inside out, the two SEALs lift him up and place him in the trunk of the Pontiac. They shut the lid and lay the keys on the rear of the car.

With that, Whyte pulls out the satellite phone and dish and punches in the code to Naval Command. Whyte passes on the information including the street name where the warehouse is located. Diamond and the SEALs hoof it on foot for another mile. Now they are well inside Baghdad. The sun is coming up; the day is getting hotter and hotter.

Three Navy SEALs and a US Marine in desert camouflage fatigues will stick out like a sore thumb if the Iraqi Army comes around any corner. They knew they had to get inside a building, undercover, hidden away for the next day. Diamond and the SEALs approach the rear of a seven- or eight-story building, with an empty swimming pool. The building and the pool are relatively new, and from the map, Diamond and Whyte can tell it's a recently built hotel. Diamond and the SEALs walk past the pool; no one is around. They enter the rear of the building and start up the stairs. When they get to the main level, one floor up, Whyte opens the stairway door to look down the hallway. It's clear. Given that it's about six o'clock in the morning, it appears no one is around. Richard enters the hallway and looks at the registry on the far wall. From the names, he supposes it's a combination hotel and office build. The top floor office is owned by a company called Universal Exports, and the sixth floor has offices from a cable news organization CNC, News of the World.

Back in the stairwell, Lieutenant Diamond and SEAL Team One climb their way to the roof, pry open the door, and try to find some shade so they can get some sleep. If it works out well, this could be the point from which they do their work, either tonight or tomorrow night. Diamond sets one of the team members as watch and tells everyone else to get some rest. The elevator and stairwell shaft are in the center of the roof. On top of the elevator and stairwell shaft are several satellite dishes, painted white with big letters in torch red—"CNC"—with the words "Cable News Corpora-tion" beneath.

Occasionally, either Diamond or Whyte look over the edge of the roof. The office hotel is the largest building for several blocks in any direction, so no one can look down on them. The street seems relatively deserted with little auto traffic and no foot traffic. Whyte and Diamond open laptops and login to the GPS system so that the Navy knows exactly where SEAL Team One is. Diamond and Whyte also pull up the best maps of Baghdad that they have. These maps identify approximately 100 government and military buildings. Whyte and Diamond get oriented. From their vantage point, they can clearly see about half of their potential targets.

Richard checks his watch. It is now about eight o'clock. Whyte is on the satellite phone advising NavCom that SEAL Team One has the package and is waiting to meet their contacts on the ground. It's difficult to hear on the satellite phone, but Whyte understands that their contact is on its way to meet them at their location. Their orders are to just hang tight.

About an hour later, the roof top door begins to open slowly. Gibbs, Miller, and Whyte turn and take aim at the door. Slowly, another US Navy SEAL appears.

Password Foxtrot. Password Foxtrot says the gentleman as he exits the stairwell and steps onto the roof.

"Response Rabbit hole. Response Rabbit hole. Glad you're here. I'm Sergeant Whyte, and this is Lieutenant Diamond."

"Nice to be here. Sorry we didn't get to meet at the drop point in the desert, but that location was covered by the Iraqi Guard. My name is Captain Steve McGarrett."

"Are you alone?"

"No, I have a guide, a local man. He's downstairs in the lobby waiting for the falafel shop to open. We've been on the move all night."

"Okay, Captain. Here's what we have for you. Four sets of the latest night vision goggles, two sets of laser assist aiming devices, and two GPS laptops that sync up with the laser guidance. Everything is packed in these two backpacks. The batteries are charged and the top face of the laptops are solar panels. When fully charged, you should have about three days before you need to charge them again."

Just then, one of the other SEALs hand signals. He points over the edge of the roof, holds up four fingers. Everyone scrambles over to the edge of the roof and peeks over. Below is a Toyota SUV about a block away. Four Iraqi policemen are out of the truck and walking toward the building. As they walk, they're opening doors to other buildings and looking in windows.

"Captain McGarrett. How much confidence do you have in your guide sitting down below waiting for tea and breakfast?"

"He should be fine. But what are our options if they take him. Hopefully they don't sweat anything out of him in the next day."

"That's not an option," says Diamond. "McGarrett, you and me are going down the stairs to see if we need to take control of this."

With that, Richard and Steve McGarrett pull out their .45s and head down the stairs quietly but quickly. When the two of them reach the bottom of the stairs, they open the door to the hallway, slowly peering out. They don't see anyone. The lobby is empty.

The lobby is not ornate by American standards. It has a black and white tile floor and several white columns with arches. Large glass windows and a glass door define the breakfast shop. Arabic writing with English translations are written on the windows—"Breakfast and lunch specials, drinks, and bread."

"Where's your man," whispers Richard.

"I have no idea," says McGarrett. "I left him right here."

McGarrett pulls out his walkie-talkie and contacts Whyte. "Whyte, what's going on from the roof?"

Whyte answers, "All four policeman are in the building, nobody else is on the street."

"Okay. Let's go back up to the roof and see if we can figure out what our next move should be," McGarrett directs Diamond.

Steve and Richard work their way back up the stairs stopping at each floor to open the door and look up and down the hallway. When they get to the seventh floor, they see that the door to Universal Exports is open. One of the policeman is standing in the doorway with his back to the hallway. Diamond and McGarrett can hear the policeman talking to the people inside. From what they make out, inside is at least one man and one woman with British accents.

Just then a commotion breaks out. Steve and Richard close the door quietly and quickly; they ascend the stairs to the roof. When they get on the roof they advise Whyte and the other team members that it looks like all hell's about to break loose on the seventh floor.

Just then, the door to the rooftop starts to open. The SEALs instinctively turn and raise their weapons. Into the sunlight emerges an Iraqi civilian with two policemen by his side, each gripping him by his arms. As the policemen enter the sunlight from the dark stairway, they raise their free hand to shade their eyes. It only takes the SEALs two shots—Boom! Boom!—and the policemen drop.

"Okay, team. Two guys cover the top of the stairs. We may have two more cops coming up any minute now. Whyte, you and I will go over the parapet edge of the roof to the seventh floor and see if we can surprise these guys from behind."

Corporal Miller unrolls some rope out of his backpack, tosses it over the edge and braces himself against the small parapet that surrounds the roof. Richard Diamond holsters his weapon and is over the roof parapet and down on the seventh-floor balcony in no time. Whyte is just starting over the roof as Richard lands on the seventh-floor balcony. In the room, he sees a tall gentleman dressed in a suit, his hands held high above his head. A few feet away is one of the Iraqi policeman with the woman that they had heard earlier. Across the room near the door is another policeman.

Diamond pulls his .45 and fires through the sliding glass door at the policeman by the hallway door. Two shots ring out, and the glass door in front of Diamond shatters. The Iraqi policeman grabs his chest and falls out the door and into the hallway. The second policeman grabs the girl with his left hand pulling her toward him, grabs his side arm with his right hand, and aims it directly at Diamond. Bang! Bang! Two shots ring out. The tall gentleman in the suit has pulled out a semi-automatic pistol and fired two shots, hitting the policeman and dropping him in his tracks. The young lady screams and takes a couple of quick steps away into the arms of the tall gentleman.

Richard enters through the shattered glass of the sliding door.

With his gun trained on the tall stranger, Richard says, "Drop it." The tall stranger holds the gun facing up in the air, slowly opens his left coat lapel and returns the gun very slowly to its holster.

With a British accent, the tall stranger says, "Nice shooting. But now you're aiming at the wrong fellow. I'm on your side."

Richard holsters his .45 and asks, "Miss, are you hurt?"

"No, I'm fine. Just a little shaken up," says Penelope Cash as she extends both hands and grabs Richard's left hand with both of her hands.

"How do you do?" says the tall gentleman. "My name is Brady, James Brady. And this is my secretary, Ms. Cash."

"Nice shooting, Mr. Brady. I wouldn't have expected that from a civilian."

"Well, we here at Universal Exports try to be prepared. It's a dangerous country, you know. In my other life, I'm known as Commander Brady, His Majesty's Royal Navy."

"Just the same, hand it over," Lieutenant Diamond says as he extends his empty hand. Brady carefully reaches into his shoulder holster and withdraws the gun, handing it to Lieutenant Diamond. "What are you carrying, Brady?"

"A Walther PP K, 7.65 mm semiautomatic."

Lieutenant Diamond clicks the safety to the on position and places the small gun in his pocket.

From the hallway, McGarrett and Gibbs enter and drag the dead policeman's body into the room and shut the door behind them. From the balcony, in walks Sergeant Whyte.

"Brady is that really you? You may not remember me, but we worked together on a NATO task force training exercise in Hawaii last year," says McGarrett.

"Why, yes, that's right. So nice to see you again, Captain McGarrett. I see you do get around."

"I might say the same thing for you, James. You're out of uniform and, I might add, a long way from England."

"Yes, I am. I'm in the Naval reserve, but my real job is vice president of Universal Exports. I'm here in Baghdad getting ready to set up a processing plant for mineral spirits, turpentine, solvents, paint thinner, that sort of thing."

McGarrett looks directly at Richard. "Diamond, sorry to leave you in such a mess, but I have to go. I have an appointment, as you know, later tonight. I must be in my location before that. Commander Brady, good luck to you. Take my advice. You and your secretary should get out of Baghdad as quickly as possible."

With some regret to see Steve McGarrett leaving, Richard says "Okay Steve, get your equipment from the roof and make your way to your spotter post. If this war does start tonight we will need you and the equipment up and ready to go. "

With that, McGarrett salutes quickly, shakes Richard's hand, and exits the door into the hallway. McGarrett take the stairs back up to the roof in order to meet back up with his guide and to get the night vision googles and laser guided targeting equipment. Loaded down with equipment McGarrett and his guide trudge down the stairs, across the lobby and out onto the street.

Richard keeps a look out the window and eventually sees McGarrett and his local guide exit the building. McGarrett and the guide walk across the street, load the equipment into the trunk of the car and climbs into a dark-green older model Mercedes-Benz four-door sedan. They drive down the street, make a left-hand turn down the alley, and disappear.

Richard looks back at Brady and Miss Cash. "My apologies for the inconvenience, but I'm going to have to insist that you two remain here for the next day or two. No phone calls, no outside contact with anyone."

Richard turns to Sergeant Whyte, "Sergeant, see if you can find an empty room, not too far away, to hide these two bodies. Take their weapons and their radios and their IDs. They might come in handy." Whyte and Gibbs start to drag the bodies out the door and down the hallway as they hunt for an empty room.

"Oh, and Sergeant, check for the keys to their SUV. We're going to have to move it; hide it somewhere.

# CHAPTER 6

# The Drive through Baghdad

The door to Universal Exports opens quickly and the two Navy SEAL team members, Whyte, and Gibbs walk in and close the door behind them. In their hands are keys, radios, side arms, the policeman's IDs, and a handful of money.

"Well, what do you have there?" asks Diamond.

"Looks like these guys had about 6000 in euros and about 1000 dinar in their pockets. That's a lot of money for a couple of cops on daily patrol."

"It looks like these gentlemen were up to no good; most likely extorting money out of foreign tourists or businessmen. Okay. Let me have that money and the keys to the truck. Check the two guys up on the roof, and see if they have anything that would be helpful. May I have a radio also? Okay. I'm going to go hide this truck, and I'll be back as soon as I can. Sergeant, leave one guy down here with the two civilians. See that they don't make any phone calls, and I'll be back," Diamond spoke in rapid succession.

Richard walks out the door, down the hallway, and presses the button for the elevator. He takes the elevator down to the lobby and exits out the front door, slowly looking in both directions to make sure it's all clear. He walks down the street quickly and hops in on the driver's side of the Toyota.

Richard begins to think, *How far away do I have to move this to be safe? Can I get it hidden away in an empty garage somewhere?* He drives down the street makes a left-hand turn and starts down the alley that McGarrett and his guide took. Richard drives for a couple of blocks, all the while searching for a garage that looked deserted. No luck. Now three blocks away, he pulls the Toyota up to a relatively large street. Approaching from the left side is an Iraqi Army truck with a machine gun mounted in the truck bed. As the truck pulls in front of Richard they look directly at him sitting in the driver's seat of an Iraqi police SUV. Diamond sees the surprised look on their faces.

The truck comes to an abrupt stop about 30 feet past Diamond, with the tires screeching in protest. The gunner in the truck bed losing his footing and tumbling down to the truck bed. The man in the passenger seat leans way out his window and shouts instructions to the man as he scrambles to his feet and gets behind the machine gun in the truck bed. The man arming the machine gun pulls back the arming lever and rotates the machine gun as far as he can. Because of the position of the truck, he can't turn the gun on and rotate it far enough to get a shot at Richard.

With no choice but to make a run for it, Diamond floors the gas pedal, takes it out onto the street, and makes a sharp left-hand turn, trying to outrun the Iraqi Army. Richard hears the pop…pop…pop of the machine gun and the squeal of the tires as the truck turns around in the street and accelerates after him. Diamond has about a 100-yard head-start but doesn't know where he's going. He takes on more gunfire as he looks in the rearview mirror. The machine gunner is getting better at his aim the longer he shoots. Bullets rip through the back of the Toyota. The rear window and tailgate shatter, then the left side window shatters. Diamond tries to swerve right and left hunting for an exit out of this big street and into an alley.

Finally, he sees a tiny alley coming up on the right-hand side. He makes a sharp turn sliding into the alley with the Toyota scattering trash cans and debris. Diamond can't keep this up for much longer. He must figure out a way to make a stand or get rid of this truck on his tail. The Iraqi Army truck makes the turn into the alley, running over the scattered trash cans. More gunfire comes his direction, ricochets off the buildings that makeup the confines of the alley. The sound of the big 50 caliber is deafening in the confines of the buildings that make up the canyon of the alley.

One block to go and another street is coming up. Diamond pulls into the street, slams on the brakes and does a J turn so that he is now facing the alley way. He leans out the driver side window with his .45 in both hands. As the Iraqi truck exits the alley, Diamond fires two shots, both hitting the machine gunner; he grabs his chest and falls out of the truck and into the street as the truck screeches across the street and over the curb.

Diamond is now sitting on the windowsill of the driver's side looking over the roof of the Toyota. The Iraqis have pulled out their side arms and are aiming them at Richard. Diamond continues to shoot, killing the passenger where he sits as the driver gets out of the truck and takes a position where Diamond does not have a clean shot. Diamond roles backward out of the SUV and onto the ground. He pats his pocket to make sure he has at least two more clips. Diamond releases the clip in his .45. As it drops out, it hits the ground and rolls slightly away from him. He quickly shoves in another clip and clicks the weapon into firing position. He begins to fire at his adversary once again. With the best burst of speed he can muster, Richard dashes across the sidewalk and crashes through the door of the closest house. Shots from the Iraqi soldier hit the wall next to Diamond as he crashes through the door.

Diamond goes to the window and looks back to see if the Iraqi is following him or staying put. He's staying put, but it looks as if he's on the radio. *This is not going to end well if this guy can get back in touch with the rest of the Iraqi Army*, Diamond thinks. He takes careful aim inside the truck at the radio. Two quick shots—Boom! Boom!—both take direct hits on the radio. As a good hit, sparks fly out of the radio, which begins to smoke. Diamond sees the guy throw the mouthpiece to the radio across the truck and into the passenger seat.

Now Diamond must get elevation. He can't get a good shot from where he is. Diamond dashes up the steps to the second floor and takes a quick look out the window. In the room is a civilian mother holding a baby in her arms. She is clearly frightened and trembling; crouched in quivering ball in the corner of the room. Richard points out the door with his left hand as he motions with his gun in that direction. The woman's dark eyes get big, she nods. The frightened woman scampers out the door, clutching her baby in her arms, holding the baby ever so tightly. The mother and baby are crying.

Diamond breaks out the window with a chair and throws the entire chair out the window. The chair and broken glass fall to the sidewalk below. The chair breaks apart and glass shards scatter on the sidewalk below.

As one last move, Diamond grabs a fistful of the money that's in his pocket; it looks like about half of his stack, maybe 3000 euro. And throws the money out the second-floor window. The wind swirls between the alley in the street as the money floats down over the SUV, with some of it reaching the Iraqi Army truck.

As Diamond surmised, the Iraqi reaches into the bed and grabs some money. As more money floats down, Richard thinks, *Will he do it again? Will he take one more chance?* Yes! He reaches over the truck bed. Diamond shoots and hits him in the head, one shot. He falls dead, slumped backward past the truck and up against the building.

*Best money I ever spent* Diamond thinks as he races down the stairs and back into the street. Richard walks across the street to find the SUV is still running. He climbs in and drives calmly, slowly making a turn up another alley and finally finding an empty garage. Diamond pulls the SUV into the empty space, leaves the rest of the money strewn over the front seat and walks out the back of the garage into the alley. The garage doesn't have a door to close, but maybe, just maybe, this hiding place will do.

Richard starts to jog back up the alley. Eight, seven, six blocks to go. Back at the hotel, Richard looks across the street from his hiding place in the alley. Richard is out of breath and breathing heavily. It all looks clear and quiet. It is now about ten-thirty in the morning. With the all-clear, Richard jogs across the street through the main door to the hotel. Richard crosses the lobby's black and white tile floor and starts to climb the stairs to the roof. The falafel shop is still closed, and the lobby's front desk has the gate drawn.

# CHAPTER 7

# The Cable TV News Show

As Diamond reaches the landing for the sixth floor, he can hear a great deal of commotion coming from the hallway. Three or four people are talking with American accents. Richard opens the door from the stairwell to the hallway a crack and observes the hallway. At the other end walking in his direction is an American cable news crew. Their torch red windbreakers are clearly marked in large white letters—"CNC Cable News Corporation."

A gentleman is out in front with a microphone in his left hand. Following behind him is a cameraman and a sound-man. The cameraman caries the camera in one hand, the soundman has a backpack on and a rolled up wire extension in one hand. Richard eases the door closed and waits in the stairwell behind where the door will open. One minute later, the door opens and the news crew enters, still talking to each other. " I tell you I heard all kinds of commotion this morning, coming from the seventh floor. There is something going on and we are going to get it ." says the leader of the pack as he enters the stairwell.

Diamond pulls his side arm and points it at the gentleman with the microphone.

"Good morning. I see everyone's in fine spirits and ready for a walk upstairs."

The entire news crew stands transfixed on the landing, everyone looking directly at Diamond's .45 automatic.

The gentleman in the lead puts both of his hands in the air, the microphone still gripped in his left hand. "Good morning, indeed. My name is Fox Donner. I'm the bureau chief for CNC cable news. This is my crew." Both of the crewmembers nod their head politely at Richard, giving the appearance of two bobblehead dolls.

Fox Donner is about 45 years old with graying hair and glasses. He wears a full beard and mustache, well-trimmed. He has kicked around the world news community for the last 10 years. He has a pleasant voice and a calm demeanor, which lends itself well to being a studio anchor. But something must've gone wrong in his career, because now he's reporting in a hot, sweaty desert town far from home, rather than sitting behind a desk in an air-conditioned studio back in the United States, eating in fine restaurants and drinking expensive wines.

"Yes, I've seen you on TV at home. My name is Lieutenant Diamond, USMC, and I'm afraid you've stumbled into an operation that you cannot broadcast or let anyone know about for the next several days," Diamond says as he points to his name on his fatigues with his left hand. "I'm going to have to ask you to step upstairs to the seventh floor. I'm also going to need to take your camera and recording equipment."

"Just a minute. You can't do that. We are a United States news organization."

"I'm afraid I can, and I will do that," Diamond retorted. "You will remain quiet, cooperative, and do as you're told. Okay, everyone one more flight up." Diamond points the .45 up the stairs. The three men trudge up the stairs slowly, deliberately, and quietly with Diamond following behind them. In the hallway on the seventh floor, Diamond points toward the offices of Universal Exports.

The news crew and Diamond enter the offices. Sitting on the leather sofa at the far end of the office is James Brady and Miss Cash. Brady has loosed his tie and unbuttoned the top button of his finely pressed white shirt. James rises as the news crew and Richard enter the room.

Gibbs is sitting behind the desk with his feet propped up on the desk and his rifle nonchalantly laying across his lap. As Diamond enters the room Gibbs stands up and trains his weapon toward the news crew. Fox Donner and his crew repeat their movements from the stairwell—three men standing in the room with their hands in the air.

"As you were, Corporal. Where is Sergeant Whyte?"

"J W is up on the roof, sir. I can call him and have him down here in one minute."

"Thanks, Corporal."

Diamond turns his attention back to Fox Donner and his news crew, as Gibbs talks on the walkie talkie. "Step over here, gentleman," Richard says as he points his .45 to the far side of the room. "Put your hands down. You look ridiculous."

Fox Donner and his news crew walk over to Brady and Cash and begin to introduce themselves, just as Sergeant J W Whyte enters the room.

"Sergeant, we've got civilians coming out of our ass, this whole operation is FUBAR before it even gets started. Contact SECNAV and see if they can give us some general direction as to what to do with the civilians, other than shoot them," Diamond orders. "Tell them we have two Brits, one of which is a British Navy reserve officer, and three Americans from a cable news crew. See what they say."

"Yes, sir, I'm on it," Whyte says as walks over to the desk where Gibbs is standing.

Richard turns his attention to the CNC news crew. "Okay, Mr. Donner. Who else is in your office down on sixth floor?"

"Just one other person. She is our producer."

"Is she American or a local?"

"She's American, only our driver is local, and he is not working today."

"Okay, then. You're going to call her on the phone and ask her to come up to Universal Exports on the seventh floor."

Gibbs gets up and moves around to the front of the desk, handing the desk phone to Fox Donner. Donner presses the number for his office and waits for his producer to answer.

"Hello, Megan? It's me. Can you come up to the seventh floor, the offices of Universal Exports? I need you to take a look at something for me." With that Donner hangs up the phone.

Penelope Cash leans over and whispers into James's ear, " what is FUBAR" ?

"American slang for things are not going as originally planned. " he says with a sheepish smile.

# CHAPTER 8

# Nighttime in Baghdad

The civilians, James Brady, Penelope Cash, Fox Donner, Megan, and the news crew are quietly sitting on the couch and chairs on the far side of the offices of Universal Exports. The light in the offices are dimmed. Gibbs continues to sit behind the desk with his feet propped up on the desk and his rifle across his lap. The wind is blowing through the sliding glass door that was shattered by the gunfire; the sheer curtains flap in the breeze. A dry hot desert wind.

On the roof, Sergeant Whyte and Lieutenant Diamond and the other Navy SEAL have their equipment open and are looking over the roof parapet with the night vision goggles. Both Sergeant Whyte and Richard look at their watches: it's ten o'clock PM. Whyte is on the laptop computer tapping away with two fingers. Diamond is looking over the edge of the parapet and holding what appears to be a futuristic rifle. In fact, it is a laser targeting system used to identify targets.

The first group of targets that will be hit will be identified by SEAL Team One and struck by cruise missiles fired from U.S. Navy warships somewhere in the Indian Ocean. As Richard points the targeting laser, Sergeant Whyte taps away on the laptop. High above the Iraqi desert flies a US AWACS communications plane. Onboard this plane are sophisticated communications and computer equipment, which are capturing the GPS location of every targeted Iraqi government and military building that will be hit by US warplanes. These locations will be transferred to Navy Command, then to B1 bombers launched from Germany and Italy, and B-52 bombers that have launched from the United States and have already refueled in midair. These long-range bombers will now know the exact locations to drop their munitions for saturation bombing.

Richard talks into a headset that is attached to his helmet, "This is groundhog, okay, okay. Target number one is lit up and ready, over." Richard takes aim at a nondescript government building approximately one-half mile away. On the top of the building is the elevator shaft; it sticks up above the regular roof by about 10 feet and is located in the center of the building. The roof of the building has about a half dozen satellite dishes aimed in different directions. Richard trains the laser directly on the elevator shaft. On his laptop, Whyte sees that the AWACS crew has captured the location of target one and gives Richard the thumbs up. Richard looks at his map and points the laser gun at another government building. Within ten seconds, Whyte again gives Richard the thumbs up.

*AWACS, inside the computer room at 45,000 feet*

Airmen sit quietly at their desks, pouring over computer screens as a number locations come up. The men have on headphones. Silently, they acquire target after target. The airplane engines drone in the background.

*US NAVY Fleet, at sea, at night*

The darkness is broken as multiple cruises missiles light up the decks of the US Navy destroyers Burke and Stout. Only one nautical mile away, the elevator of a US Navy Aircraft Carrier lifts Navy jets to the flight deck. A few minutes later, with a great roar, the jets take off, and turn north toward Bagdad.

*Back on the roof top, two hours later*

Richard looks at his watch; it's just past midnight. They have been setting targets for just over two hours.

Coming back into his headset, Richard hears the scratchy voice of a US Navy pilot. "This is Eagle One. Target number one A is locked on and ready. Birds away. Birds away."

Sergeant Whyte looks over at Richard and gives him two thumbs up as he looks at his laptop. About 20 seconds later, the building that was the communications headquarters for the Iraqi Air Force is hit with the laser-guided munitions. The large explosion lights up the night sky, and the big boom shatters the quiet of the night.

Diamond looks at his map, which is held down on his knee. He leans over the parapet and takes careful aim with the laser-guided rifle another time. "This is groundhog. Okay. Okay. Target number two A is lit up and ready, over," Richard repeats into his microphone.

Back in Richard's headset is the scratchy voice of the same U.S. Navy pilot, "This is Eagle One. Target number two A is locked on and ready. Birds away. Repeat, birds away."

Whyte looks over at Richard and again gives him two thumbs up as he scans his laptop. About ten seconds later, a second building about three-quarters of a mile away is hit with a laser-guided munition. On the other side of the city, far away on the horizon, other buildings are hit that were targeted by SEAL Team Six. The night sky ignites with flashes of light, then the quiet of the night is broken by big explosions. Steve McGarrett and his SEAL Team Six lighting up the other side the city.

Richard and Whyte continue targeting government and military buildings throughout their section of Baghdad, while staying in radio and computer communications through AWACS with both US Navy warplanes and US Navy warships. US Navy warships are launching cruise missiles, about one missile every five minutes. Richard and Whyte continue the laser-guided targeting and recording of targeted locations using GPS. Within a few minutes of each fixed-building target, the sky is lit up with either a cruise missile strike or a laser-guided munitions strike.

About a half hour into the nighttime operation, the Iraqi Army starts to place mobile rocket launchers throughout the city of Baghdad. SEAL Team One is continuing to look for these operations through their night vision goggles. After the location of the truck-mounted rocket launchers and radar guidance systems are located, Richard targets them with the laser-guided system and Whyte plugs their GPS coordinates into the laptop. It only takes a few minutes of communications from the AWACS to the US Navy warplanes above to target these mobile rocket launchers and radar guidance systems with air-to-ground missiles.

Far on the other side of town, government and military buildings are being struck with regularity. These other buildings are being targeted by Steve McGarrett and his SEAL Team Six crew.

The Iraqis load missiles into the mobile launchers and get off no more than a half a dozen shots before the mobile launcher is struck and blown to bits. This operation is repeated nearly 50 times over the next hour and a half.

Richard and Whyte continue this operation for about three hours. In that time, they have guided about 200 laser-guided munitions from US warplanes and cruise missiles from US ships, which lock onto their targets with nearly 100% accuracy.

There would be no hiding the news that the United States and its allies have attacked Baghdad, Iraq in response to the terrorist's assault on the World Trade Center. With this thought in mind, Richard and Whyte head downstairs to the seventh floor. Richard and Sergeant Whyte enter the offices of Universal Exports, where they find everyone wide-awake and sitting quietly in their chairs.

Fox Donner rises as soon as he sees Lieutenant Diamond and Sergeant Whyte enter the room. "Look here, Diamond," he starts with great agitation. "You can't keep a great news organization silent on this war forever. I absolutely demand that you return my equipment and permit us to at least get this on film so we can put it on the news later."

"Donner, you and your news organization are free to report anything that's happening now, provided you do not mention in any way, shape, or form this location or that the US Navy SEALs are located here inside Baghdad," Diamond replied.

"Okay. We can live with that. Guys, grab your equipment and head back to our offices. Let's go! Let's go! I want film of all the big explosions we can get our hands on, and I'll start working on the monologue to cover it." Fox Donner and the CNC news crew grab their equipment and hustle out into the hallway and down one flight of stairs to the sixth floor.

In five minutes, they have a news camera setup out on the six-floor balcony aimed at downtown Baghdad, with the buildings that Richard and Whyte have identified and the U.S. Navy now has locked into their GPS along with the GPS locations that were targeted by Steve McGarrett and his Navy SEAL Team Six on the other side of Baghdad.

Now the US Air Force flying high above is dropping saturation bombing on the targeted locations to destroy the buildings, the infrastructure, and other early targeting devices held by the Iraqi Army.

*On the sixth floor in the offices of CNC cable news*

"Good evening, America and the world. This is Fox Donner in Baghdad reporting for CNC World News. Tonight, the United States military and its allies have launched a massive air campaign against the Iraqi Military here in Baghdad. The footage you are now seeing shows numerous government and military buildings across Baghdad being hit with what appear to be smart bombs, by US Navy and Air Force warplanes from high above, as well as cruise missiles and air-to-ground missiles. There has not been a lull in the attack, which has now lasted more than three hours. As you can see from our film footage, the Baghdad Army is fighting back furiously with surface-to-air artillery, machine guns, and surface-to-air missiles. At this point, we can report that we have no confirmation of any US warplanes being shot down. The tracer bullets being fired by the Iraqi Army are lighting up the sky, but we have not seen any evidence that they have struck any US warplanes in their counteroffensive.

"From our vantage point here on the sixth floor of this hotel, we can feel the concussions when the large explosions that have hit nearby. The sound of the explosions is deafening. We can report that no less than 100 buildings appear to be destroyed or on fire at this time. This attack comes as a response to the terrorist attack on the World Trade Center. The United States has made no secret that military action could come as a last resort in response to the terrorist attack on 9/11. We are going to send you back to our studio in Atlanta now. We will continue to cover this air campaign here from Bagdad and provide updates throughout the night. This is Fox Donner reporting live from Baghdad."

"Cut. That's a wrap," says Megan. The photographer takes his handheld camera off his shoulder and the soundman puts down his equipment. Out on the balcony of the six floor of CNC news, the crew still has a camera sitting on a tripod aimed at downtown Baghdad, recording all the footage they can of the night sky being lit up by the United States military.

Up on the seventh floor, Sergeant Whyte receives a call on his satellite phone. "Yes, sir. Yes, sir. I got it. I'll relay the information to Lieutenant Diamond," Sergeant Whyte says as he clicks the phone off and puts the phone back in his knapsack. "Lieutenant, that was SECNAV. Our targeting operation here is complete. SEAL Team Six will handle all targeting from this point forward. The Air Force is going to do a flyover tomorrow during the daylight hours to assess the damages."

"Okay, Sergeant. Put one man on the roof on watch. It's almost four AM now. Everyone else get some sleep and be prepared to move out in the morning as soon as we get definitive orders and directions," Diamond replied.

# CHAPTER 9

# The Hunt

S ergeant Whyte and Lieutenant Diamond are sitting on the floor of the offices of Universal Exports, with their backs resting up against the wall. Their helmets are off and sitting nearby, their rifles are propped up against the wall adjacent to each man within easy reach. Whyte has the laptop on his lap with the screen open and glowing a dim blue as he leans over to talk to Lieutenant Diamond.

"Lieutenant, SECNAV is pulling us off our forward targeting duty. They say SEAL Team Six can handle it from here. After the reconnaissance flyover, the B-52s will hit the targets that need to be hit again."

"What, then, is SECNAV asking us to do next?"

"The brass wants our team to track down those trucks we saw at the warehouse two days ago. Locate them for targeting before they can be used against our ground troops. SECNAV believes that what we came across was WMDs, either chemical or biological shells. They have daylight satellite images of the truck convoy heading north out of Baghdad for either Mosul or one of the other northern cities or possibly even for transport into Syria and maybe even Russia."

With Diamond's Texas drawl more evident than usual, he said, "So, let me get this straight. The brass wants us to track down some trucks headed north in a country that's half the size of Texas. I'm from Texas, boy, and it's a big place. What the hell makes the brass even think we can find these damn trucks?"

"I have no idea, Lieutenant, but they're going to give us the last known location and direction. We have to scrounge up some transportation and figure it out from there."

"Okay, we can use that Iraqi Toyota SUV I hid in the garage, assuming it's still there."

Lieutenant Diamond and Sergeant Whyte get up, place their helmets on, and strap their rifles over their shoulders.

Lieutenant Diamond walks across the room as Brady and Miss Cash are just waking up from sleeping on the two leather couches on the far side of the room.

"Mr. Brady, all hell's going to break loose again tonight, just like last night. I don't know how safe you will be here. A bad shot by either the US or more likely a bad shot by the Iraqis could hit this hotel. I recommend that you and Miss Cash either get underground as far as you can or head south toward the US lines for safety."

"Thank you, Lieutenant. I have a house about a mile from here. Cash and I will head there and stay undercover. I hope this will be over soon." James stands up and picks up his suit jacket draped neatly over the back of the sofa. He puts his jacket on and extends his hand to help Miss Cash off the couch.

"Oh, Mr. Brady, here. You might need this." Richard reaches into his pocket and extracts the Walter PP K. Richard hands the gun, butt first to James. James takes the gun from Richard's hand and places it in his shoulder holster. In his Texas drawl, Richard looks directly at Miss Cash. "You all be safe now."

Miss Cash looks directly back at Richard. "Don't worry, Lieutenant," she says in her British accent as she reaches into her small clutch purse and pulls out a small semi-automatic pistol, a Beretta .22 caliber. "We here at Universal Exports believe in being prepared." She walks over to her desk and picks up a business card sitting in a cradle in front of her desk. Penelope turns the card over on its back and writes her phone number on the back of the card.

"Lieutenant, I want of thank you and your men for everything you've done. If you're ever in London when this is over, give me a call. My private line is on the back. I look forward to hearing from you." With that Penelope and Brady exit the offices and walk down the hall. Richard looks at the number on Penelope's card and places the card in his pocket. Without realizing it, Richard has a big grin on his face, looking every bit the Cheshire cat in camouflage.

James Brady and Penelope Cash exit the elevator on the first floor of their building. They walk across the black and white tile floor to the double glass doors of the entrance. They look both ways carefully out in the street then leave, making a right-hand turn and starting to walk down the street briskly.

"James, do you think they'll find out we are tapped into the CNC's satellite positions?"

"I doubt it, Penelope. They are not looking for that. The best thing we can do now is get home and send this information to the Foreign Office. We'll have to send it over the shortwave radio in code."

"What about driving to the oil refinery about 200 miles north of here? There is a satellite dish and secure link to the Foreign Office there."

"It's too risky. There's a high chance we would get stopped by a checkpoint along the way. No. Our best option is to send this information up the ladder as soon as possible. We'll see what the big bosses say and go from there."

"What is with giving your phone number to Diamond?"

"Don't worry, James, I gave him my cover phone number from the agency. If he calls, it will be recorded, and we will trace the line. Who knows? Having a contact inside the US Navy SEALs might be useful someday."

"Well, Penelope, you may be right about having a contact, but did you notice Diamond did not have a US Navy SEAL patch? The other three were US Navy SEALs, but Diamond was USMC."

James and Penelope continue to walk briskly as they approach a large stucco home surrounded by a six-foot high white stucco wall. On the top of the six-foot-high wall are two-foot-high steel pikes sharpened to a point at the top. They approach a wrought iron gate with a ten-digit number key panel to the side. James presses numbers into the key-pad as Penelope pushes the gate open. They quickly go inside, shutting the gate behind them and tugging on it to ensure is locked.

James and Penelope enter through the front door of the house, closing the door behind them. They quickly go upstairs to the master bedroom and cross the master bed-room to the master closet at the far end of the room. Inside the master closet Brady separates some clothing to expose a hidden door. James and Penelope open the hidden door and extract a small, shortwave radio. James turns on the shortwave and the yellow glow from the dial lights up the closet.

"Penelope, what is the kilo hertz for today's date?"

"980 KHS, James. Here….I've started to code the message."

"Thanks. I'm going to give the Foreign Office hell for this, if and when we get back in London."

James looks at the yellow legal pad Penelope is writing on and begins to type on the keyboard. His two fingers type as fast as Penelope can print the message.

*Back at the offices of Universal Exports*

"Okay, Sergeant, you and I will rotate guard duty on the roof, and let the other guys get some sleep," orders Diamond. "We head out as soon as it gets dark. Get on the laptop and send the message to SECNAV that we need all the data they can give us on the location, direction, and number of trucks we're looking for."

"Okay. I'll see what information the brass can get us," confirms Whyte as he opens up the laptop and starts typing two-finger style.

"Corporal, go back to the bodies of the four Iraqi policemen that you hid away. Take off their uniforms and bring their clothes, ID badges, guns, and anything else that might be helpful back here."

The Iraqi policemen were stashed in a storage closet just down the hall. It only takes the Navy SEALs a few minutes to take their uniforms, guns, radios, ID badges, and the money left in their pockets. They bring everything back to the offices of Universal Exports.

When they return, Richard walks over to the door, closes it with a solid click, and locks it. He then strolls across the room casually to where the two leather couches are at the far side of the room. He takes off his helmet, sets it on the floor, and props his gun up against the arm of the couch. He undoes the hooks to his body armor, removes it, and rests it on the floor next to his helmet. He lays on the couch on his back, staring at the ceiling, trying to sleep. Richard drifts off to sleep thinking of Margie back in Virginia.

## CHAPTER 10

# The Trek North at Night

It's nightfall on the second day of the Iraqi War. As the sun sets and the temperature begins to drop, Lieutenant Diamond and SEAL Team One ready for their new mission. Sergeant Whyte sits at the desk where Ms. Cash once sat. The laptop is open and the blue glow is reflected on Whyte's face.

"Okay, Lieutenant, SECNAV has sent the information they have on the movements they want us to track. They re-tasked a satellite and got some satellite imagery of a relatively big truck convoy heading north on the main road to Mosul. But they lost them at nightfall. So, they could be anywhere. Mosul or even into Syria."

"Thanks, Sergeant, here's a working plan. We go back to the garage where I hid the Iraqi Police SUV. If it's still there, we take it and head north along the same road to Mosul. Let's gear up and get to that police vehicle before all of Baghdad is out assessing the damages from last night."

As darkness falls on the streets of Baghdad, SEAL Team One takes the stairs down to the lobby level of the hotel. Richard and Sergeant Whyte look out the door to the lobby. Everything looks the same except the glass door to the falafel shop is ajar.

Lieutenant Diamond and Sergeant Whyte turn and whisper the information about the door ajar to the other members of the team. Just then they hear a noise coming from the falafel shop. As they peer through the crack they've created in the door leading to the lobby, Richard sees a mother and two children leaving the falafel shop with their arms loaded with milk, bread, rice, and other groceries. The woman and the two children exit out the front door of the hotel.

Diamond, Whyte, and the two Navy SEALs exit the stairwell and walked toward the front door of the hotel. Richard reaches into his pocket and extracts the 1000 dinar and hands the money to Gibbs.

"See if you can find us some traveling food in the falafel shop. Make it quick."

Gibbs takes the money, opens the door, and walks into the shop, while the others wait by the front door of the hotel. In only a minute or two, Corporal Gibbs comes out of the shop with his arms loaded down with food.

"I got us pita bread, hummus, figs, dates, water and grapes. I tucked the money into the counter. We are good to go. Most of the food is gone out of the shop, the shop keeper must have stayed home when all the shooting started."

Richard and his three SEAL companions exit the hotel carrying their equipment on their backs along with the Iraqi police uniforms tucked under their arms. They walk across the street and down the alley. Once in the alley, they quicken their pace. Seven blocks later they are approaching the garage where Richard hid the Iraqi SUV. As all of them look in the darkened garage, the SUV is illuminated by their flashlights. It is still there with the rear window and one of the rear side windows shot out and the passenger side mirror gone.

*Back at CNC cable news, Baghdad*

Fox Donner is sitting behind his desk writing on a yellow legal pad. His producer  looks over his shoulder. Megan says, "That sounds good, Fox. That should be about three minutes of airtime. Get ready, everyone. At two minutes past the top of the hour, we're going live back to Atlanta."

Just then the door to their offices open and two Iraqi Army officers enter the room. In broken English, the officers ask what they are doing and whether they have a permit to be filming and broadcasting.

Fox Donner rises from behind the desk. "Yes, we have a permit. We are the only news agency telling the world how fiercely Baghdad and the Iraqi Army is fighting back."

The two Army officers walk across the room and step out onto the balcony where the tripod and camera equipment are still set up. They don't touch the camera equipment, but they look at it carefully and closely from all angles. The two Army officers reenter the room and look at the sound equipment that is sitting on the floor.

Fox Donner turns to Megan, "Get our permit out of the file cabinet and show it to these gentlemen."

Megan walks to a small to file cabinet and extracts two pieces of paper with golden seals at the bottom. "Here, sir, please look at this. We are fully permitted to film anywhere in Iraq. We have a permit from the Iraqi Ministry of Communications and from the Iraqi military."

Two Army officers walk briskly to Megan and snatch the two pieces of paper out of her hand. They give the two pieces of paper a cursory review, and in broken English they turn and speak to Donner. "Have you seen any other Iraqi police or military in this building today?"

Donner puts both of his hands out from his side as if to say to his staff that he's going to answer the question. "No. You are the only Army officers we've seen all day. But, we've been staying in our offices as you might imagine for safety reasons. I don't believe there's anyone else in the building except us."

The senior Army officer looks at the other officer and says, "Leave them. We have other offices in the buildings to check." The two officers hand back the paper to Megan and walk out the door.

Donner puts his index finger up to his lips, signaling to his staff that they are to be quiet. He then whispers to them, "They are going to find the four dead cops on the seventh floor in a few minutes. We can't run now. We will look complicit as hell. And, how far could we get? All hell's breaking loose outside. We just stay here, be calm. Remember, we don't know shit. We didn't hear anything; we didn't see anything."

*Back in the garage*

A dry desert wind blows down the alley. In the distance a dog could be heard barking in the darkness, a big angry dog from the sound of it. "This is our ride, gentleman, search around and see if there are any gas cans nearby," says Richard as he fans his flashlight beam around the expanse. Without warning, another flashlight beam pierces from the adjacent house. A civilian, an older man, speaks to himself in Farsi. Richard and the SEALs turn their flashlights off and hunker down behind the SUV as the old man enters the garage. Whyte grabs the old man from behind, places him in a choke hold, and holds the arm with a flashlight against the man's chest.

The old man begins to speak this time in French. "S'il vous plait! S'il vous plait!"

Richard shines his light on the old man. "Do you speak English?"

"Yes, I speak four languages," says the old man.

Whyte loosens his grip, allowing the old man to stand upright. The old man places his hands in the air still holding onto his flashlight. Sergeant Whyte frisks the old man with his hands. "Nothing on him. He's clean."

"Are you from the American army?" asks the old man. Richard doesn't answer but simply shines his light on the patch of old glory on his shoulder.

"America! I love America!" The old man says, still holding his arms above his head. "I did not know what to do when the police truck showed up in my garage. I thought I should call the police, but then the bombs started falling out of the sky. So, I did nothing."

With Richard's flashlight beam still shining in the man's face, Richard says, "Well, you won't have to worry about what to do with the SUV. We're going to take it off your hands."

"You will need extra petrol," says the old man, and he points to a large gray metal cabinet on the far side of the garage.

Two Navy SEALs go to the metal cabinet and opened it. Inside are two, five-gallon red gas cans. One of the SEALs pops the top on both cans and takes a sniff. He looks back at Richard and Whyte and gives them two thumbs up. Richard looks inside the SUV on the passenger seat.

"What happened to the money that was on the seat?" Richard asks of the old man.

"Well, money is money, and this is Baghdad," he says as he shrugs his shoulders, grinning from ear to ear.

Richard opens the door to the SUV and looks in the glove compartment. "Just what I was looking for—a street map of Baghdad and the surrounding area."

Whyte, still holding the old man speaks up, "What should we do with him?"

"Let him go," says Richard, and Whyte releases the old man. The old man puts his hands down and turns around and hugs Sergeant Whyte.

"You cannot stay here. Too many of the neighbors will report you to the Army or to the police. You must go," the old man says to Whyte after the embrace.

"What's your name, old man?"

"My name is Professor Hamid Fossil. I was a professor of languages at the American University in Baghdad many years ago. Now I run a grocery store. I know the forces of evil here in Bagdad, government thugs, criminals, drug traffickers. "

"Professor, go back in your house and go back to sleep. You have seen nothing, and you do not know anything." Richard says directly to the professor. And with that, the old man walks out of the garage and back toward his house. He walks slowly.

Richard thinks to himself, *forces of evil, my ass; petty crooks with thoughts of grandeur. Well they are about to meet the United States Marine Corps.*

"Okay, boys, let's get the gas in the back, along with any equipment we will want. Let's load up and head north," Richard says as he starts to walk around to the driver's side of the vehicle. He hands the half-folded map over to Whyte as he climbs in the passenger seat. Gibbs and Miller load the equipment through the broken rear window, including the two gas cans. When everyone is in the SUV, Richard shifts into reverse and backs out into the alley.

Richard starts driving up the alley at a slow pace without turning on the lights. "Pass the food around. Everyone should eat. I, for one, am starved."

The four men chow down on the bread and hummus as they drive slowly through the streets of Baghdad. The figs and dates are fresh and good. The grapes are large, plump, red seedless grapes.

# CHAPTER 11

## The Road to Mosul

With the roadmap unfolded, Whyte holds it at arm's length up against the dashboard. He gives directions to Richard on how to get to the main road out of Baghdad heading north to Mosul. It takes them about 20 minutes to drive through the streets of Baghdad until they reach the main highway heading north. As they drive through Baghdad, the city behind them is being hit by cruise missiles and other guided munitions. The sky lights up with the antiaircraft fire from the Iraqi Army. Bright streaks of tracer fire and antiaircraft rocket fire light up the sky.

SEAL Team One sees very few civilian cars, but those they do see are all exiting the city heading in the same direction that Richard and Whyte are driving. Some of the civilian cars and small trucks are loaded with family possessions, mattresses strapped on roofs, and beds of pickup trucks loaded with furniture and children. Richard drives, drawing as little attention to himself as possible.

The coordinates SECNAV supplied for the last-known position of the truck convoy is about a two-hour drive north of Baghdad. The little bit of traffic on the main road north out of Baghdad begins to slow down. Richard can see what appears to be an Iraqi Army checkpoint about a quarter-mile ahead. Four guards stand in the road, and a portable generator on the side of the road powers a light stand. The Army guards appear to be stopping vehicles and checking identification. For all Richard and Whyte know, they could be extorting money out of the civilians fleeing Baghdad.

Richard leans over and taps Whyte on his shoulder. Whyte looks at Richard and gives him the thumbs up, letting him know that he sees the threat ahead. Richard pulls his .45 from its holster and clicks the safety to the off position. The two SEALs in the back seat, Gibbs and Miller, ready their weapons with a distinct click as they switch their weapon safeties to the off position. The law firm of Gibbs and Miller are about to lay down the law to some unsuspecting Iraqi Army members. As they approach the checkpoint, Richard slows the SUV so the guards can see it is clearly marked as a Baghdad police vehicle. For just a moment, the two guards closest to Richard relax and point their weapons toward the ground.

Richard floors it and accelerates as fast as he can. With his .45 out the driver side window, he begins firing at the two guards on his side of the car. From the back seat, Gibbs and Miller raise their weapons, and with pinpoint accuracy shoot the two guards on the passenger side of the car. The last remaining Iraqi Army guard, continues to fire at the SUV as it speeds off into the night. Gibbs and Miller pivot and fire out the broken rear window of the SUV. The fourth and final Iraqi Army guard is hit and goes down.

Seeing that all the guards are dead or wounded and lying on the ground, Whyte says, "We're okay, Diamond. We made it through the checkpoint." Just then on the side of the road, two head lights emerge and begin to chase Richard and SEAL Team One into the pitch-black desert night. The SUV is giving it all it can; the motor is screaming. The two big headlights behind them are gaining on them fast. The pursuit vehicle puts on its high beam lights. Gibbs and Miller begin to fire at the vehicle chasing them. Their bullets are clearly bouncing off the vehicle's armor. Gibbs exclaims clearly, "We're being run down by some sort of armored personnel carrier or an armored light truck. They're going to catch us in about two minutes."

Just then, the vehicle behind them opens fire with a rocket-propelled grenade. With a small explosion, the Toyota is lifted onto two wheels and spun sideways. The SUV spins out of control as it is struck by the pursuit vehicle. The impact tears the driver side door off and strikes Richard hard on his left side. Richard's .45 falls out of his hand and helplessly hits the pavement and disappears into the darkness.

Richard regains control of the SUV and tries once again to accelerate away from the pursuing light truck, which they now know is a Mercedes-Benz SUV. The Mercedes is sideways in the road, but it takes it only a moment to turn. Its engine roars as it pursues Richard and SEAL Team One.

Richard shouts orders to the two Navy SEALs in the rear seat. "We are outgunned and out horse powered. We have to get this guy off our tail. As soon as he gets close enough, throw the two gas cans out the back. Let's see if we can light him up!"

In the late-model Mercedes SUV, two Iraqi Army officers pursue SEAL Team One at a high rate of speed in the darkness of the desert night. The officer in the passenger seat leans out the window holding his second shot with an RPG. Just then, Gibbs and Miller from SEAL Team One throw out the two five-gallon gas cans from the broken rear window. One gas can hits the ground and bounces up against the grill of the Mercedes. The second can bounces slightly higher in the air and lands on the SUV's hood, opening up and spilling gas over the hood and through the open window of the passenger side. All of this happened just as the Iraqi Army guard is ready to fire his RPG. The spark from the fire of the RPG ignites the fire on the hood and the inside of the SUV. The RPG shot is no good; with all the confusion, the shot goes way off into the air. With the Mercedes on fire, the driver slams on the brakes and turns the wheel. The SUV crosses the road and crashes into the ditch on the far side. The driver, badly hurt and on fire, jumps out of the car and stumbles onto the desert sand. His passenger, unable to get out, remains inside, screaming as the Mercedes continues to burn. Finally, two big explosions come from inside the Mercedes. With a big fireball, the Mercedes and the passenger inside are turned into a burning mass.

Richard is hurt. He feels sharp pain in his left leg, but continues to drive into the darkness. After two hours of steady driving, SEAL Team One is at the last known location of the truck convoy. It is now past midnight in the desert, and the only lights provided are the two beams of light from the SUV. Whyte is busily tapping away on his laptop, when the light on his satellite phone turns from red to blinking green. Whyte picks up the satellite phone and turns it on. The scratchy voice on the end of the phone speaks right away. "Sergeant, we have some additional information for your team regarding your location of interested. We have a location for the cell phone number you provided us last night. It's pinging off a cell tower at an oil refinery with a private airport about 40 miles from your current location. Turn off the road you're on now and head north northwest about 40 miles across the desert. I am sending the coordinates to your computer now."

"Thank you very much. We will be at that location in an hour. We'll call in when we arrive. We are going to need transport out. Our current ride is on its last legs and will not make the trip back to Baghdad or back to anywhere," says Whyte. He then switches off the satellite phone.

SEAL Team One drives slowly through the desert. Richard looks down at the gas gauge. "Guys, we are almost out of gas. Unless we run across to an all-night gas station in the middle the desert, this is a one-way trip in this SUV." As Richard shares this information, the SUV approaches a paved road, which proceeds in approximately the same direction that Richard wishes to go. He turns onto the paved road and drives another 20 minutes, when he comes upon a large sign and a fence with a gate across the road. The sign says "Trans Global Oil" in big letters across the top of the sign along with the company's logo. In smaller letters, there is a note of the phone number to call for the refinery two miles ahead. At the bottom of the sign, in smaller letters yet, "In partnership with Universal Exports."

# CHAPTER 12

# Trans Global

Diamond sits in pain in the driver's seat of the stolen Toyota SUV Police car. With the driver- side door torn off, the desert sand buffets his face. The headlights illuminate the chain link fence and gate that block the road.

Sergeant Whyte and one of the Navy SEALs get out of the SUV and walk up to the chain-link fence that stretches across the road. The gate is closed with a large chain and padlock. The Navy SEAL takes careful aim with his rifle from about 10 feet away. One shot rings out, and the padlock is busted. The two men remove the chain and swing the double gate open. Richard pulls the SUV forward slowly and the two men get in. Richard turns the headlights off and drives up the road with only the parking lights giving a dim yellow glow out in front.

With his left leg injured badly, Richard drives with his right foot for both gas and brake. He hasn't told the other team members, but the pain in his left leg grows worse by the minute. It doesn't take long for the SEAL team to approach the Trans Global refinery. They see the lights of the refinery just over the horizon. Richard turns the lights out completely and drives to the ridge of the hill very slowly. They stop the SUV just prior to the ridge of the hill, and all the men get out with their weapons drawn. Richard winces in pain as his left leg touches the pavement and cannot support him.

"Sergeant, I need some help over here. I'm injured," says Richard with a grimace of pain. Sergeant Whyte and Gibbs come to Richard's aid. Richard puts his arm around Whyte's shoulders, and together they walk to the ridge of the hill and look down upon the Trans Global refinery and a makeshift airfield. Portable lights mounted on poles are powered by small generators. The lights are all aimed at the makeshift landing strip. Viewing the scene through their night vison goggles, Richard and his team can see several trucks parked with their rear tailgates open facing the airfield in the darkness beyond the portable lights. Richard and SEAL Team One stand behind a small outcropping of rocks looking through binoculars at the trucks and airfield below.

Just then, an old prop cargo plane with Syrian markings on the tail approaches the landing strip and lands in a single pass. The plane turns at the far end of the landing strip and taxis back toward where the trucks are located. The plane is about the size of a DC-3, but Richard does not recognize the plane's manufacturer—it's Russian or possibly Chinese. As the cargo plane comes to a complete stop, the side door opens and two men in military uniforms jump out of the plane and onto the tarmac. Soldiers on the ground approached them, and they greet as friends. The pilot and copilot appear to be Russian based on their uniforms. The trucks parked just outside of the glow of the portable lights are now started up and maneuvered back toward the cargo plane. As many as 20 men in military uniforms walk out of the darkness and begin to unload the trucks directly into the cargo plane. Through the binoculars, Richard and Whyte can clearly see that they are loading the same boxes that SEAL Team One observed back in the Baghdad suburbs. The boxes vary slightly in size but are clearly marked on the top with the same distinctive color coding.

Richard sits down and extends his injured left leg with some difficulty. "Corporal, see what we have in the medical kit for my leg," Richard directs.

"Yes, sir, let me have a look at that," he says as he kneels and examines Richard's left leg.

"Lieutenant, it looks like you have a compound fracture in the lower extremity of your left leg. I can splint this for you and wrap it tightly to relieve most of your pain. I can also give you something for the pain," he says as he unfolds the medical kit and starts to work on Richard's leg.

"I think I need a second opinion. " Richard exclaims with a smile and a Texas drawl .

" yes sir. , ...you're ugly and can't drive for shit " Gibbs and Richard burst out in laughter.

It takes about three or four minutes for the Navy SEAL to splint Richard's leg with two rigid pieces of plastic and wrap it with a bandage and tape.

Richard gives the corporal two thumbs up as he finishes the bandaging. "Thanks, Corporal, that should get me home."

Just then Whyte approaches the SEAL team members carrying the satellite phone and a holster and handgun. "Diamond, here's a side arm from the Iraqi police, out of the back of the SUV. I think we should call in this location and our findings to SECNAV and get additional guidance on our mission." Whyte hands the side arm and holster to Richard. The gun is a Makerov 9 mm semiautomatic, fully loaded. Richard takes the gun and puts it in his holster that previously held his Colt .45. He tosses the Makarov holster on the ground.

"See if you can get SECNAV on the line," Richard says to Sergeant Whyte.

Sergeant Whyte sits on the ground behind the rocks with his laptop open, as he two-finger types in all of the information he can remember regarding the location and what SEAL Team One has found. It only takes a few minutes for SECNAV to answer back.

In the blue glow of the Whyte's computer, the answer comes back, "Cannot risk air strike on possible chemical, biological, or nuclear weapons. Close air support and transport out is two hours away. Maintain your position. If possible, attempt to disrupt and disable enemy."

"Okay, Sergeant Whyte, here's the plan. You and the law firm are going to work your way around to the back the warehouse and try to gain entry. Determine if there is any information regarding the exact nature of the munitions being shipped out and where they're being flown. Look for any sort of manifests or shipping documents. I'm going to stay here with the sniper rifle. If all goes well, in two hours we're going to get air support. Until that time, we're only going to engage the enemy if he realizes we're here. It will take them some time to load up this transport. If we have to, we'll try to take the plane out just before it takes off or just as it gets in the air.

But we are not going to let two Russian pilots fly off with a load of chemical or biological weapons back to Syria or even back to one of the Russian republics."

"Okay, Lieutenant, we'll be back in touch by radio as soon as we are in position at the back of the warehouse." With that, Whyte and SEAL Team One check their gear, strap on their night vision goggles to their helmets, and then trek off into the darkness of the desert.

Richard props the sniper rifle with its scope up against the rocks. He pulls out his binoculars, leans on the rocks, and looks down on all the activity at the warehouse. The loading continues as they haul one box at a time from the back of the trucks to the side door of the aircraft. From there, the heavy boxes are hoisted up into the airplane and disappear into the cargo hold. The Russian pilot stands by with a clipboard in hand, checking off each box as it is loaded into his aircraft.

Richard looks at his watch. Approximately an hour has passed since SEAL Team One walked off into the desert darkness. Just then Richard's radio buzzes. He picks it up, clicks the mute button to the off position, and places the handset at his ear. From the other end, Whyte comes in loud and clear.

"We are in position and have breached the rear door. We've located the offices, which appear to be empty. We're going in."

Richard answers with approval, "Good work men. Only one hour until air support arrives."

*Inside Trans Global Industries*

With night vision goggles on, the trio of Navy SEALs quickly searches the offices of Trans Global Industries. Outside, about 50 feet away, three trucks sit half loaded with unknown munitions. Gibbs and Miller gather up laptops and desk computer hard drives while Sergeant Whyte searches the paper files for anything that look like manifests. Whyte whispers to the others, " I wish Big Mack was here, I can't tell what I'm looking at. Most of this stuff is written in Farsi or in Sanskrit for all I know, but I think I found some Russian documents. "

Gibbs answers back quietly, "we need something to carry this stuff in, start looking for a large trash bag or something."

Miller calls out quietly over his helmet mounted microphone, "I found a bag in here. It's a Russian duffel bag, half full of clothing."

Sergeant Whyte looks over at The Law Firm and gives them a thumbs up as he gathers reams of documents.

Back at the spotter location, Richard listens in over his helmet head set.

Just then, Richard hears a noise that he didn't want to hear. Richard hears the whine of the aircraft's props starting up on the runway. All of Richard's senses are heightened. He picks up the sniper rifle and leans over the rocks, carefully looking through the scope. Richard trains the crosshairs through the cockpit window of the airplane. He can see the Russian pilot climbing into his seat; the copilot is already seated and at the controls. The men on the ground have closed the cargo hold bay door. The loading trucks, which are now half-empty, have their headlights on and are driving slowly away from the runway and back into the shadows behind the glow of the portable lights.

Richard picks up the portable radio and presses the signal button. Inside the warehouse, Sergeant Whyte and SEAL Team One hear Richard's voice in their helmet headsets. "Sergeant, I'm sure you can hear that cargo plane has started its engines. He's going to be taxiing down the runway making a turn and coming right at me as he takes off. Get into position, because in about two minutes, maybe less, I'm going to take out pilot and copilot."

"Roger that," comes back Whyte's voice to Richard. "We are on the first floor and will be in position in thirty seconds."

The four-engine prop plane with Syrian tail markings and two Russian pilots begins to taxi to the far end of the runway. The plane goes into the darkness beyond where the portable lights shine, but the vehicle has its running lights and headlights on. Richard can now hear the engines come to full throttle as the plane comes out of the darkness and accelerates almost directly toward him. Richard takes careful aim with the sniper's rifle, putting the crosshairs directly on the pilot's chest as he begins to pull back on the stick. Richard squeezes the trigger slowly, one shot rings out, shattering the windshield on the pilot's side and hitting the pilot in the chest. The plane's nose tips down, and the plane begins to veer off the runway.

Richard quickly shifts his focus to the copilot. The copilot grabs the yoke and begins to steady the airplane. He also pulls back hard on the stick as he tries to get the heavily laden plane up in the air. This time, Richard pulls the trigger twice; two shots both hit the copilot.

With the pilot and copilot slumped forward against the controls, the plane makes a sharp right-hand turn. The plane strikes one of the portable light stanchions with the portable generator at its base. The plane's wing clips the light pole in half, and a ball of flames bursts out of the plane's wings. The plane is now spinning clockwise with one broken wing dragging on the ground.

The plane spins and runs off the runway coming to a stop as it crashes into one of the half-empty trucks. The men around the trucks scramble, running as fast as they can to escape the danger. Richard looks through the sniper rifle and can see an Iraqi Army officer shouting orders to the 20 or so soldiers scattered throughout the landing area. The soldiers on the far side of the runway scramble from one temporary light location to the next, turning off the generators as they go. Once the generator is turned off, the lights begin to dim and are completely dark in about five seconds. The lights on Richard's side of the runway are left running. Those lights shine on the Iraqi soldiers, who are now hidden behind the dim light stanchions, the portable generators, and several of the trucks. Through his scope, Richard can see them clearly. Richard takes aim at the officer who shouted orders and is now crouched behind a truck. Richard's shot is low and ricochets off the hood of the truck. The soldiers down on the runway are having trouble locating the shot's trajectory because the lights on the far side of the runway are facing them, and Richard is well hidden.

From one side of the darkness comes a Toyota pickup truck with a machine gun mounted in the bed. With great speed, the Toyota dashes across the airstrip and beyond the lights into the darkness. The Toyota turns and heads up the road toward Richard. Richard begins to fire on the Toyota as it races toward him. The machine gunner in the bed opens fire on Richard's position. Richard ducks behind the rocks as near misses shatter the top of the rocks. Richard pulls a grenade, his only one, from his belt. He pulls the pin and lofts the grenade gently but carefully and accurately into the air toward the Toyota pickup. In a single blast, the grenade goes off in the air just above the driver's side of the pickup. The blast shatters the window and sends the truck sideways at a high rate of speed into a roadside ditch. The truck crashes, sending the machine gunner over the edge and onto the ground.

*With any luck*, Richard thinks, *they're both injured enough that they will stay put.* The two men are in a ditch approximately 10 yards from Richard's position and on the other side of the road. He can hear them moving around, but he cannot see them.

*Down at the airstrip*

Down at the airstrip, the Iraqi Guard are getting organized. With their officer as point man, they start to cross the airstrip and race up the road that leads to Richard's position. From behind them out of the darkness, the three men of SEAL Team One open fire with pinpoint accuracy. The Iraqi Guard and the officer turn and charge the gunfire coming out of the warehouse. The firefight is a furious gun battle, but in the end, all the Iraqi Guard that stayed to fight are lying on the runway dead. Several Iraqis flee the airstrip, running into the desert darkness and disappear.

Richard hears the two Iraqi guards that were in the Toyota pickup talking on a radio. He cannot make out what they are saying, but they talk furiously. Then over the horizon about a half mile away, Richard sees lights coming down the road toward him. It's the same road that Richard and SEAL Team One used to arrive at their current position. Based on the number of lights, it is either more shipments of weapons in trucks, or it's a column of Iraqi Guard. In either case, they're going to arrive on top of Richard in one or two minutes.

Richard hobbles back the Toyota SUV and climbs into the driver's side with no door. He starts the Toyota up and takes a quick glance at the gas gauge, which reads E. Richard puts the sniper rifle on the floor of the passenger seat with the rifle pointed upward. With the lights off, Richard floors the Toyota and heads for the runway about 100 yards below him. As Richard passes the Toyota pickup in the ditch, the two Iraqis come out from behind their hiding place with guns drawn. Richard pulls the Makerov 9 mm side arm from his waistband and fires at them as he speeds by. The Iraqi soldier standing near the rear of the pickup is struck in the left shoulder. The other soldier quickly ducks down behind the pickup for safety as shots from Richard's Makarov ricochet through the truck bed. Richard continues downhill to the airstrip as fast as he can, knowing that the Iraqi Army is two or three minutes behind him.

# CHAPTER 13

# Air Support

Richard drives onto the runway and comes to a stop. Out of the darkness comes Whyte, Miller, and Gibbs at a slow jog in a crouched position. Sergeant Whyte is out in front by about two paces. Miller and Gibbs are carrying a large duffel bag between them. The duffel bag appears to be quite heavy, and Gibbs and Miller strain to keep it off the ground. Miller and Gibbs climb into the rear of the Toyota, placing the duffel bag between them, as Whyte walks around the front of the SUV.

"What's in the duffel bag?" asked Richard just as Whyte opens the passenger side door.

Miller and Gibbs answer almost in unison. "Two laptops and a bunch of files that look like shipping orders and manifests in Russian."

Suddenly, shots hit the Toyota on the passenger side. The Iraqi Army men that ran into the desert darkness are now crouched behind the light generators on the far side of the runway. Sergeant Whyte starts to climb into the Toyota when Richard pulls his side arm.

"Get your ass down!" Richard orders as he aims the gun at the Iraqi Army personnel. Richard starts firing and continues to fire until the Makarov is empty. Some of the shots ricochet

105

off the generator base, but two of the three Iraqi Army guards are hit and fall onto the tarmac. Gibbs and Miller now have their rifles aimed out the window of the backseat. They fire at the third and final Iraqi soldier. He is hit and goes down.

Whyte, slumped over the passenger seat, leans back and pulls the passenger door closed. He's been shot. Richard can't tell where, but there's blood oozing down the sergeant's side from under his armored vest.

"Thanks, Richard, you really saved my ass," says Sergeant Whyte. Just then Richard sees the lights of the trucks at the top of the hill about 100 yards away. As Richard begins to pull down the runway and look for an escape route, an ear-splitting roar from an airplane flashes overhead. Out of the darkness at 20 feet above Richard and the SEAL Team One is a US Hercules C-130, coming in for a landing at about 100 miles an hour. Richard pulls the microphone from his helmet close to his lips, and tries to contact the plane's occupants. As the plane passes over them, the rear loading ramp begins to lower as the plane meets the tarmac. The wheels touch the ground with a big screech and a burst of blue smoke. Richard accelerates the Toyota SUV as fast as he can. About 50 yards behind him is the Iraqi Army, now shooting at them with small arms fire. Miller and Gibbs instinctively turn and return fire out the rear window.

Richard accelerates as fast as a little Toyota will carry them and looks at the gas gauge one last time. The needle is below empty; they're running on fumes. Richard accelerates as fast as he can toward the braking Hercules. The Toyota tops out going more than 100 miles an hour as Richard hits the rear loading ramp and pulls into the back of the giant aircraft.

Richard slams on the brakes, and the truck comes to a screeching halt midway inside the big aircraft. Corporals Gibbs and Miller exit the rear of the car, each on his own side, and with purpose walk toward the rear of the plane. It's as if they had just gotten out of a limo parked at a sporting event, and they were walking in to watch a ballgame. They each eject the clip out of their rifle, and slam a new clip into place.

Gibbs and Miller, standing on opposite sides of the C-130 transport ramp, train their rifles on the enemy below. Each man begins to fire clear, controlled shots. On the tarmac below partially lit by the portable lights for the landing strip, they see a truck with surface-to-air missiles pulling into position. Gibbs and Miller take aim at the truck and with their last few shots try to disable the portable missile launcher. The truck driver is hit, and several soldiers on either side of the truck are also hit, they are down bleeding Iraqi blood onto the tarmac.

Meanwhile, Richard gets out and in great pain walks around the front of the car holding onto the hood. Richard opens the passenger side door and reaches in to help Sergeant Whyte out of the vehicle.

At this point, the pilot and copilot realize this is not a landing but a touch and go. They push the controls forward on the big C-130, and it lifts off into the darkness. The C-130 is now taking ground fire from below. RPGs come at the plane, but do not appear to do any damage. The RPGs explode, sending shrapnel pelting the underbelly of the plane and the rear loading ramp. As the Hercules climbs, the Toyota begins to shift and drift backward toward the still-open ramp. Richard puts both arms around Sergeant Whyte and holds on as the truck continues to drift backward. Whyte falls out of the seat, and both he and Richard fall backward onto the floor of the plane. The big Hercules is now gaining altitude as the Toyota falls out of the rear of the plane and into the desert darkness with its lights still on.

*Inside the C-130 cockpit*

The pilot and copilot of the C-130 are experienced US Air Force pilots. Upon approaching the Trans Global airfield, they got a perfect view of the column of Iraqi soldiers trapped on the road approaching the airfield. Their quick thinking in lowering the tailgate to pick up everyone that needed to be evacuated was the perfect move. They open the rear ramp and slow the plane as slow as they could go and still maintain control. They hit the runway and apply the brakes with every hope that the SEAL team they were sent to evacuate could make it on board. They realize they could not land and load up the much sought-after munitions.

The C-130 accelerates and makes a sharp bank right when an alarm goes off in the cockpit. "We've been acquired. We've been acquired. They have locked on to us," the copilot says to the pilot. "Rocket fired. Ten seconds to impact."

"Launching countermeasures. Launching countermeasures. Countermeasures away," responds the pilot.

*The view from the cargo bay*

The Toyota truck falls away, getting smaller and smaller as gravity pulls it toward earth. The flash of the countermeasures is a short, bright light outside, as the countermeasures fire backward out of the plane and fall toward the desert floor. About a mile away, a mobile rocket launcher flashes, and its trail appears as a surface-to-air missile speeds toward the Hercules.

The missile gains speed, gaining on the Hercules, and it is only a matter of 10 seconds. Brace for impact! With a big explosion, the missile actually acquired the Toyota SUV along with the countermeasures the pilots launches. The Toyota SUV is blown out of the sky.

## CHAPTER 14

# Helicopter Gunships Arrive

The rear tailgate of the big Hercules closes as the plane continues to make a right-hand bank. Richard looks out one of the side windows to see the Iraqi column of trucks on the road approaching the airfield. Out of the night, the truck-mounted rocket launcher explodes into a ball of fire. The fire of the crashed Russian air cargo plane and the fire of the rocket-launching truck illuminate the desert night sky. Richard sees two AH-1 Cobra attack helicopters, as well as a third helicopter. The two Cobras are fully armed with air-to-ground missiles. Both pilots are experienced combat pilots, and in no time the aircraft let loose all their weaponry on the column of Iraqi trucks. In a matter of minutes, the two Cobras have decimated the entire column. Cobras are taking small arms fire and are responding with their 20 caliber Gatling gun fire. The tracer bullets show the helicopters laying waste to everything in their site. With that, the two Cobras turn and accelerate to head for home. They did their job and did it well. The Iraqi Army column is on fire, with dead and wounded strewn all over the desert.

The big Hercules lumbers on into the night heading south over the top of Baghdad, which is now on fire in more than 100 locations.

Richard helps Whyte to his feet and helps move him to the front of the airplane, where he can be strapped into a seat. Miller and Gibbs walk from the rear of the plane toward where Lieutenant Diamond and Sergeant Whyte are seated.

"Great shooting you guys, I would go into combat with you guys anywhere, anytime," compliments Richard.

"That's what we're here for, Lieutenant."

"What happened to the duffel bag with the laptops and paper data in it?" Richard inquires.

"Bad news, Lieutenant. The duffel bag was still in the backseat of the Toyota. It's now blown all to hell," explained Miller.

"Oh, shit. What should I tell the brass in my report?"

"I don't know, Lieutenant. You can either write it up just like it happened, or you can tell the brass nothing. Like it never happened. Like we didn't find anything, and it didn't get blown out of the sky," replied Gibbs.

"Maybe you're right. Most of the munitions, whether chemical or biological, are gone. Flown out before we got here or are burning up on the airfield below us," concluded Richard.

Sergeant Whyte moans and begins to unbuckle his bulletproof vest. Gibbs and Miller approach Sergeant Whyte and lay him on the deck as the Hercules drones on south toward safety. Gibbs and Miller cut away the sergeant's camos and begin to administer first aid.

"Hang on, Sergeant, we'll be on the ground in no time. You are not hit too badly. It looks like a through and through," said Gibbs.

# CHAPTER 15

# Inside the US Field Hospital

U S Navy Seabees are as busy as they can be erecting concrete walls with barbed wire tops around a temporary US military hospital and air field. This field hospital will take in US military wounded and wounded enemy combatants. Army intelligence officers and US Navy Intelligence officers mill around outside the plywood and canvas tent hospital waiting to interview both captured enemy combatants and US armed service personnel who may have vital information regarding enemy troop movements or tactics at the front. This hospital was later reconstructed inside Baghdad in an area that became known as the Green Zone much later in the war.

Helicopters come and go at a furious pace, landing approximately 50 yards away in an open desert field. A makeshift landing strip is beyond that. From there, the wounded are transported by Jeep, ambulance, or on wheeled gurneys and taken directly to the hospital's triage.

Standing just inside the triage area is US Navy Nurse Captain Patricia Hagan. She's a cute thirty-year-old redhead standing 5 ft.4 inches tall with wavy red hair hanging just to her collar. Her temperament and personality match her hair. Her piercing green eyes survey the area. Captain Hagan selects the most critically wounded, and as she cuts their

EDWARD F. KOEHLER, PhD

clothes off for observation, she directs corpsman to wheel them into adjoining operating rooms just down the plywood hall. Several casualties are wheeled in at the same time, one of them being Lieutenant Richard Diamond with a badly broken leg. Right behind Lieutenant Diamond coming off the same plane is Sergeant J. Willard Whyte, who was wounded by gunfire. The third gurney pushed through the double swinging doors is an enemy combatant in an Iraqi Guard uniform, an officer with an apparent gunshot wound. Sergeant Whyte's bulletproof vest has been removed, as has part of his upper body clothing.

Captain Hagan looks at him and shines her small flashlight into his eyes looking for a response and dilatation. Sergeant Whyte's eyes show no response when Captain Hagan examines him. She calls out his name, but still receives no response. Captain Hagan raises a right-hand as two orderlies come into the room. Sergeant Whyte is nonresponsive. He's in shock.

"Take him down to X-ray for an abdominal picture and then OR room number two, and let's get him a pint of blood and a pint of plasma in him." she says to the orderlies very crisply and in complete command. The two orderlies grab the cart, one at each end, and turn left out the double swinging doors beneath a sign that reads, "X-ray." They move quickly, but do not hurry.

Captain Hagan next turns her attention to Lieutenant Diamond, who is lucent, alert, and clear.

"Captain, is Sergeant Whyte going to make it?" Richard asks showing great concern in on his face for his fellow soldier.

"We will know in about 20 minutes, as soon as the doctors get a look at the X-rays," Captain Hagan responds as she starts cutting up Diamond's pant leg. "What happened to you Lieutenant?" she asks.

"Car crash in the middle of the desert. I had a disagreement with a big Mercedes-Benz SUV," he responds.

By this time, Captain Hagan has cut off Richard's pants, and he sits propped up on his elbows with his bare legs sticking out of the bottom of his olive drab pants. Just then, two other orderlies walk into triage. Captain Hagan pulls out a clipboard and attaches a sheet of paper to it as she scribbles quickly and hands it to Richard. She then turns to address the two orderlies directly.

"Take him down to X-ray. The doctors will want to have a good look at his leg," she orders. Turning back to Lieutenant Diamond, she continues, "and I'll see if we can get you some pain medicine."

Just then, the enemy combatant soldier wakes up on his gurney and begins to moan. The two orderlies wheel Richard through the double doors and make the same left-hand turn toward X-ray.

Captain Hagan is dressed in US Navy nurse camouflage attire. She has a Colt .45 caliber handgun on her hip and a US Navy-issue helmet for headgear. She walks over to the enemy combatant to ensure his restraints holding him to the gurney are still attached. She wouldn't want him to fall off by accident. As she approaches the combatant, she holds her small exam flashlight in her left hand. Just as she reaches the Iraqi, he the injured combatant soldier frees his left hand from the straps that hold him to the table.

As Captain Hagan shines the light on him to check for reflexes, he reaches out and grabs her by the collar with his left hand. He pulls her on top of him, and she begins to lose her balance. He removes his right hand from the restraints, and as Captain Hagan begins to pull away, he knocks off her helmet, which falls on his chest.

Although he is in great pain and screams out, he grabs her helmet with his right hand. Still holding Hagan's collar with his left hand, the Iraqi takes a back swing with his right hand as he holds the helmet. The crown of the helmet lands crisply on Captain Hagan's right cheek; the blow is fierce, and the impact almost knocks her out and causes her to fall to the ground.

Still entangled, Captain Hagan and the enemy spill over sideways as the gurney dumps them to the ground. He releases his grip on Captain Hagan as the gurney bounces onto the floor. With both of his hands now free, he begins to undo the additional straps that hold him in place. As quickly as he can work, he releases the top strap around his chest, then reaches down lower to release the strap that holds his legs in place.

Captain Hagan regains consciousness as she rolls over and sits up. The wounded Iraqi is now free of the gurney and on his knees. He still has Captain Hagan's helmet in his right hand. He lunges at her from his knees, taking another hard swing with the helmet in his right hand. Captain Hagan leans back quickly, avoiding the hit. She screams for help.

The Iraqi gets to his feet and stumbles slightly to a small desk where writing utensils and clipboards lie. He grabs a large letter opener and moves toward Captain Hagan, who is now up on her knees. The Iraqi soldier is a big man, much bigger than Captain Hagan; in fact, he outweighs her by 100 pounds. The Iraqi soldier charges Captain Hagan, knocking her backward as he falls on top of her.

The Iraqi soldier sits upright with the letter opener in his right hand ready to stab Captain Hagan. With her right hand, she pulls her side arm. The soldier goes for the gun and grabs Captain Hagan at the wrist. As he strikes down to stab her, she blocks the strike with her left hand.

The doorway swings open abruptly. Standing in the doorway is Corporal Leroy Jethro Gibbs with his rifle slung over his shoulder. The Iraqi soldier holds Captain Hagan's wrists firmly against the concrete floor as he raises up again for one more stab with the letter opener. In one fluid motion, Corporal Gibbs unslings the rifle on his shoulder and take aim at the Iraqi. Two shots ring out, hitting the Iraqi in the chest knocking him backward. As the Iraqi soldier lies bleeding on the floor, Captain Hagan rises to her feet, puts her side arm back in its holster and retrieves her helmet.

Just then, two doctors enter the room after hearing the shots fired. One of the doctors leans over next to the Iraqi. "No need to schedule an X-ray, he's dead." The other doctor examines Captain Hagan, looking at her face where she was struck with her helmet. "You might have a broken jaw, Captain. Let's get you down to X-ray and take a look at it."

Still slightly stunned from the encounter, Patricia Hagan places her helmet on her head. "Yes, sir, I think I'm all right though. Just a little shocked." She then turns to Corporal Gibbs. "Corporal. Thanks...I owe you my life."

"No need, ma'am. Just doing my job."

Captain Hagan and the doctor walk through the double swinging doors and down the plywood hall to X-ray.

# CHAPTER 16

# The Flight Back to Germany

Two days after Richard had his leg operated on and set, he lies back on his stretcher, resting and feeling comfortable except for the pain in his left leg. Several nurses and corpsman walk up and down the aisles checking on all the wounded as the engines of the big Hercules hospital transport start to warm up.

The nurse in charge is Captain Patricia Hagan. She is in command of the other nurses and corpsman. Clearly, she has both their respect and admiration for her capabilities.

The corpsmen exit the rear of the plane, and the big ramp of the C-130 starts to close. All the injured are strapped in as the plane begins to taxi. Captain Hagan walks up and down the aisles greeting and checking on every patient. Captain Hagan asks Richard how he's feeling and if he's comfortable.

"Yes, ma'am, I'm fine. But if you could check on my sergeant over there, I would appreciate it." Richard points to Sergeant Whyte, who is one row over and a few spaces down from where Richard is positioned.

"Sure, I'll check on your sergeant. He's taken one big hit, but he's made it through initial surgery and should make the flight to Germany without any complications."

The next thing Richard realizes is that Captain Hagan is seated and strapped in up near the front of the plane, adjacent to where the pilot and copilot enter the cockpit. Several cabinets of supplies line the walls at the front of the plane, and Captain Hagan looks over to make sure that everything is secure. The four big turboprops of the Hercules begin to whine, louder and louder. The pilot releases the brake, and the Hercules starts to pick up speed, a little bumpy, then more speed. In no time, they are airborne.

About one hour into the flight, Richard wakes up from a nap and notices Captain Hagan taking a special interest in Sergeant Whyte. She doesn't look frantic, but she does look concerned. Richard sees Captain Hagan going to the supply cabinet and pulling out what appears to be plasma or some other clear liquid in a plastic bag, which she attaches to a hypodermic that is feeding Sergeant Whyte.

"Captain Hagan! Captain Hagan! What's going on with Sergeant Whyte? Is he okay," Richard calls out.

"He'll be fine. Don't worry. For some reason, he's losing blood pressure. He might possibly have some internal bleeding that was not completely resolved at the field hospital before he was discharged for transfer," she replies. " It's possible one of the cauterized blood vessels has opened up. "

The big Hercules drones on for another hour, now over the Mediterranean. Richard can see out his window and admires the clear blue water far below. Another flurry of events takes place at Sergeant Whyte's stretcher. Captain Hagan and one of the other nurses are continually checking on him. The nursing staff has reloaded the plastic bag of clear liquid to supply Sergeant Whyte with additional fluids.

Captain Hagan approaches Richard with concern etched on her face. "Lieutenant Diamond, can I speak with you for a moment? You are blood type B negative and so is Sergeant Whyte. We do not have any B negative on board in our supply, because it is a relatively rare blood type. Other than your broken leg, you're perfectly healthy and capable of giving blood," she explained. "If you feel up to it, I'd like to perform a transfusion from you, to give to Sergeant Whyte."

"Yes, ma'am, whatever you need, whatever the sergeant needs. If I can do it, if I can help, I sure will." With that, Captain Hagan and another nurse rollup Richard's shirtsleeve and set up a blood donation bag just below his stretcher. It takes less than 20 minutes for Richard to pump out a pint of B negative, and only one or two minutes more for Captain Hagan to take that pint of blood down to Sergeant Whyte and begin administering it to him.

Sergeant Whyte lies motionless on his stretcher, seemingly oblivious to the activity around him. Captain Hagan thanks Richard for possibly saving Sergeant Whyte's life. She is calm and quiet, and her pale green eyes look directly at Richard.

For several more hours, the big engines just drone on as the plane flies quietly over the Mediterranean, then over France on its approach to Ramstad Germany, US Air Force Base. As Richard looks out the window, the airbase looks just like it did a mere ten days ago. *Oh, how the world has changed,* thinks Diamond.

The C-130 lands with its usual screech of tires and puff of blue smoke. It taxies for what seems like an eternity but surely was only a few minutes. The next sound Richard hears is the big rear door opening. He sits up slightly on his elbows to look around. He sees corpsman and nurses coming in to take the wounded off for additional treatment. Nurse Hagan checks on every patient as he leaves, writing notes on charts that hang from stretchers. She repeats the same procedure for Sergeant Whyte. She adds a note to Lieutenant Diamond's chart, puts the note in the large plastic envelope and hangs the note back on Richard's stretcher.

Two orderlies approach, unstrap Richard's stretcher from its secure position, and lift him out into the hallway. As they start to carry him toward the back of the plane, Richard gives her a quiet wave and a thumb's up. She waves back and then goes on about her duties with the remaining patients.

# CHAPTER 17

# Recovery in Ramstad, Day One

R ichard wakes the next morning in a comfortable US government hospital bed, his leg in traction but feeling fine and hungry. The orderly brings a hot breakfast of scrambled eggs, sausage, whole wheat toast, coffee, and orange juice. Richard is just finishing his breakfast when he looks out into the hallway to see Sergeant Whyte being pushed by on a gurney.

"Hey, Sergeant, JW !" Richard calls out. Whyte lifts his head from the gurney and recognizes Richard.

"Hey, boys! Wheel me in there for just a few minutes. That's my lieutenant."

"Glad to see you made it," says Richard.

"Not without you. I understand you gave me some blood on the plane. Otherwise I wouldn't be here."

"No big deal. Forget it. You would do the same for me."

"They put me back on the operating table yesterday afternoon and had to stitch up one more spot. But the docs tell me I'm going to make a full recovery. I was kind of out of it on the plane. Do you remember the name of the nurse that took care of me?"

"Yes, she was a redhead named Captain Pat Hagan. Great nurse. If you get a chance, you should look her up."

"I'm going to do more than that. I want to look her up and give both you and her a well-deserved vacation."

"What are you talking about? I get all the vacation I need from the US Marine Corps. You know, see the world, and all that."

"Well, Lieutenant Diamond, this might seem hard to believe, but my father and grandfather are J. Willard Whyte the first and the second. I'm J. Willard Whyte the third. I'm going to make a couple phone calls and have my lawyer stop by to see you in a day or so. He's going to give you a card that looks like a credit card. It will have preloaded with 30 days of free lodging at any Willard Whyte Hotel around the world. It's the least I could do. You saved my life, not once, but twice. And, if I can find that little redhead nurse, I am going to give her a vacation too, just as soon as I can track her down."

"Whyte, what the hell are you doing in the Marine Corps? Get out as soon as you can and go lie on a beach somewhere, in front of one at your hotels and don't ever look back."

"Well, I joined for an adventure. I thought it was my duty, you know, and here I am. I think you may be right, I might have had enough adventure. After this is over, don't be afraid to look me up, Richard," said Whyte suddenly turning serious. With that, the orderlies wheeled Whyte's gurney out of Richard's room and continued down the hallway.

"See ya!" shouts Richard with a Texas drawl as he waves good bye to the his friend.

# CHAPTER 18

# Recovery in Ramstad.
# Day Two: Company

R ichard lies in bed propped up on his elbows with the bedside telephone sitting on his stomach. He holds Penelope Cash's business card in his left hand and the phone receiver in his right.

"Penelope, this is Lieutenant Richard Diamond. I'm in Germany and just leaving you this message to let you know I made it out of Baghdad all right. I have a broken leg and will be laid up in the hospital for a few weeks. Then I go to rehab. I hope you get this message. I'll try to call you again in a day or so." Richard hangs up the phone and places the phone back on the bedside table.

*London, in the flat of Penelope Cash*

A phone sits on the windowsill, in the eighth-floor apartment owned by Universal Exports. The view outside the window is spectacular: Big Ben and Parliament and off to the right The London Eye Ferris Wheel.

*In Ramstad, Germany*

Several people knock politely on Richard's open door.

"Can I come in and talk to you for a few minutes Lieutenant, or should I say *Captain* Diamond," says the gentleman standing in the doorway. "Richard, I have your promotion papers with me, to give to you. Captain Cole sends his best, and wishes for a fast recovery. "

As the naval officer walks closer, Diamond recognizes Captain McGarrett along with two other people, a man in a business suit and an Asian woman who hangs back at the doorway. She's also dressed in civilian clothes, her long black hair almost down to her waist. The man appears to be late thirties, maybe early forties, and the Asian woman is thirty years old at most.

"Richard...I'm glad to see you made it out of the fracas in relatively good condition," says McGarrett. "From talking to your doctors, I understand you will be in traction for your broken leg for a few weeks and then you'll go to physical therapy. It would normally be a no-brainer to do your PT at either Bethesda Naval Medical or Walter Reed," he said.

"But, I'd like to make you a different offer. We're looking for someone with your education and skill set. You have a Bachelor's degree in engineering, and you've almost completed your Master's in engineering and applied mathematics. But, I'm telling you things you already know," he continued and paused before continuing.

"Let me introduce you to Mr. Smith and Miss Jones. They have a few things they would like to share with you and get your opinion," he finally concluded.

Mr. Smith steps forward from behind Captain McGarrett and extends his hand to Richard. To Diamond's surprise, McGarrett leaves Richard's hospital room and closes the door behind him. Richard reaches out and shakes hands with Mr. Smith a bit tentatively. In his straightforward manner and Texas drawl, however, Richard says, "So, tell me. What the hell's this all about?"

Mr. Smith is dressed in a dark navy, well-tailored business suit, white shirt, and red tie. He looks like any businessman walking down Madison Avenue or Wall Street. His dark hair is neatly trimmed, and he has a modest tan.

"Okay, Diamond. Here's the short answer. We need someone in about eight to twelve weeks—maybe more, maybe less—who can pose as an engineering professor visiting a foreign country on an exchange of engineering and mathematics professors to attend a conference on ocean wave propagation and beach erosion mitigation. While there, you will present a paper that we will prepare for you on wave action and shoreline erosion. I will also need you to observe some places that you may get access to." Diamond was a bit confused, but his interest was piqued.

Mr. Smith continued. "We will provide you with a full stateside cover story, your university, previous work record, and so on. We will also provide you with an assistant, who will pose as your secretary. We will need photographs and any other additional information you can obtain of the site we designate"

Richard looks up. "This doesn't sound like US Marine Corps standard operating procedure. This sounds like you really need a spook. I'm not a spook, believe me. I'm a US Marine."

"Captain Diamond, if we thought we could get an engineering professor out of Princeton or Harvard or Yale to do this job, we would be considering them. It's not World War II anymore, even if we could recruit a college professor form one of those universities, there's no way they are going to pass the security clearance check. Patriotism at the college level is gone; now it's anarchy, fascism, socialism, and communism. God help us. But you have a security clearance, and you have skills we need. You can shoot, you can run, and you can hide when needed. We also think you won't crack under pressure. I will fully prepare you with your background. And, as I said, an assistant will be there to ensure your safety."

"Who could you possibly send with me that's going to ensure my safety?" asks Diamond.

From the doorway comes the nicest voice, someone Diamond had nearly forgotten. "Well, that would be me," says Ms. Jones as she steps forward. Diamond surveys her again; she's only medium height, maybe 5 ft. 7 inches tall. She's wearing a well-tailored suit and high heels. The skirt stops just above her knees and clings to her body like summer heat. She has a pretty face with a pleasant smile, and looks to be of Chinese-American descent. She's wearing little makeup with only red lipstick.

"Okay. Let me get this straight. I'm going to go to either Bethesda Naval or Walter Reed for recovery, and then while I'm recovering you're going to create a false identity for me. Do I have that part right?"

Ms. Jones walks to the end of Richard's bed. "No, not exactly, Captain Diamond. We want to send you somewhere else to recover, a secret location where we will prep you for the next eight weeks. Your Marine Corps records will indicate, though, that you're being treated at Bethesda Naval Medical. " Smith says, then continues.

"You, however, will be with me and the rest of our training staff, acquiring the knowledge and skills you'll need for your mission, should you choose to accept it. You won't be a direct employee of our company. For all intents and purposes, you'll keep your position with the Marine Corps."

"Well, I certainly am intrigued," Diamond finally responds. "And, could you just tell me what happens after the mission?

Mr. Smith reaches into his inside jacket pocket and extracts a small black notebook. "Sure. If all goes well, this should be a one-time deal. Then, you'll just return to your regular life in the Marine Corps as if nothing happened. Of course you can't tell anyone anything. Not a single word, ever. You're not married, so we know you will not be saying anything to a wife you don't have. Your mother is deceased, and your father is retired US Navy." Smith reels off Diamond's history with ease.

"We know your dad now works for a civilian defense contractor as an electrical engineer designing guidance systems. He has a Top Secret security clearance. You have an older sister who is married to an outdoorsman. They live off the grid; they don't even have a phone. That about sums up all your family connections and obligations, wouldn't you say?" says Mr. Smith in a matter-of-fact tone but with a smug look on his face.

"I'm thinking about getting a dog. You left that out."

"We know. A Dalmatian. But you don't have one yet, and if you do eventually get a dog, you can't tell him anything either. " Smith smiles.

"If I'm going to be out of commission for a long time, what about my car and house, and even small things like my mail, telephone, and utilities? What about my friends?"

"Don't worry about any of that, Captain Diamond. The agency will see that your car is picked up from Andrews, and we will park it in a covered garage in Washington DC. As for your house and utilities, while you're working for the agency, we will set up a bank account in your name and pay your utilities and your house payment. We will also monitor your telephone on a regular basis. When we can get to you safely, we'll relay any important messages." Smith seems to have covered every contingency. He has no discernable accent.

"Oh, what the hell. Count me in. And just for clarification, your names aren't really Smith and Jones are they?"

Ms. Jones smiles. "Good. We were hoping you would say that, Captain Diamond. Welcome to the C.I.A." says Ms. Jones as she extends her hand to Richard. "You rest up and recover for the next week or two here in Germany. We'll be in touch about your transfer to a rehab facility."

Both Smith and Jones turn their backs and leave Richard's room. The door closes slowly behind them. Richard listens to Ms. Jones's heels click down the hall until all he hears is silence.

# Bethesda Naval Medical Center, Two Weeks Later

M argie drives up the long driveway to Bethesda Naval Medical Center, makes a right-hand turn and parks her car in the visitors' parking lot. She exits her black Mercedes Benzes, locks it, and walks the short 50 yards or so to the main entrance. She walks up the outside steps of the gleaming white building. Inside the main building, she approaches an information booth, her high heels clicking and echoing through the massive lobby with every step.

At the information desk, Margie shows her Department of Defense ID badge and asks for Lieutenant Diamond, who is in rehab. "I'm looking for a Lieutenant Diamond. He was injured several weeks ago, and I understand he should be here in rehab."

"Yes, ma'am," says the nice lady behind the desk. "Rehabilitation is on the fourth floor, rear. Just take those elevators right there to the fourth floor. Sign in here, here's your visitors' pass. When you leave, please drop off your pass back here."

"Thank you," Margie says with a smile.

Margie takes the elevator to the fourth floor, the visitors' pass clearly clipped to the front of her slacks. She walks down the corridor past the sign that says "Occupational Therapy" and through the double glass doors clearly marked "Physical Therapy."

Margie is dressed in a white silk blouse and black slacks with black pumps with a short heel. Her hair is fixed and her makeup impeccable, she looks like she just walked out of a movie. Margie approaches the nurses' desk. A US Navy male nurse is standing behind the desk doing paperwork.

"Yes, ma'am. How can I help you?" he says in a thick southern country boy accent, as he looks up from his duties.

"I'm here to see Lieutenant Diamond. It's kind of a surprise. He's not expecting me."

"Yes, ma'am. One moment, please. Let me check and see if I can find him for you," he says as he scans a large sheet of paper attached to a clipboard. "Ma'am, we did have a Lieutenant Diamond scheduled for physical therapy here, but I think he was a no-show. We have paperwork on it, but he never showed up. My captain can check into that for you and see if we can locate him."

"No, that's not necessary," replied Margie. "I don't want to put you through any trouble. I just thought I would stop by and see him. I've brought him some of his favorite movies on tape." Margie opens her purse and pulls out two VHS tapes. "Perhaps some of the other wounded sailors would appreciate these movies. I have *North by Northwest* and *The*

*Man Who Knew Too Much*. If it's all right with you, I'll leave these tapes with you. Let me jot down my phone number. If Richard should become your patient in the next few days, would you please ask him to call me?"

Margie jots down her name and phone number on a small pad of paper that was on the counter. She doesn't tear the paper off the pad, but instead just extends the entire pad across the counter to the sailor.

"Will do, ma'am. Thank you. You have a nice day now."

Margie turns around somewhat disappointed that she couldn't see Richard, she retraces her steps back through the double glass doors down the hall, down the elevator, and turns in her visitors' badge at the front desk.

*Back on the Fourth Floor, Physical Therapy*

Having watched Margie leave, the male nurse flags down one of the doctors. "Captain, can you take a look at this? I have paperwork for a Marine Lieutenant Richard Diamond, but he never showed up. He was supposed to be here last week. And a nice-looking lady just showed up a few minutes ago to visit him," he explains.

"Don't worry about it, sailor, just probably a snafu. He could be anywhere. On a hospital ship recovering. Still in Germany, or maybe they're sending him down to Walter Reed. Just hold on to the paperwork. File it away. If he shows up, we will treat him when he gets here," the captain replied.

"The lady left some movies and her phone number. Believe me, he wants to have her visit him. She a stone-cold knock out."

"Take the movies down to the wards and see who wants them. Give me that phone number. I'll take care of that." The captain looks at the note, *Margie Jordan, and a Virginia phone number.*

# EPILOGUE 2

## Somewhere in Northern Europe

The air is crisp and cold; Richard rests on an outdoor chaise lounge. His left leg is still in a cast, and a pair of crutches lays on the ground next to him. Behind him on the manicured grass is a pair of dumbbells. On Richard's lap is a large three-ring binder, and another three-ring binder sits on a small adjacent table. Ms. Jones approaches down a narrow gravel path; behind her looms a very stately large home. In the distance is an expansive blue lake.

"How's the studying going Richard?" Ms. Jones says with a smile. She is dressed in a summer silk dress of daffodil yellow and sandals. Her jet black hair is braided and tied at the end with a bow that matches the yellow silk dress.

"Very well," replies Richard. "The stuff you've given me to review is easily within my capabilities based on my engineering education. When do I get to find out more information about the mission itself?"

"As soon as you're ready, Richard, but don't rush it. The mission will be ready when you are. The data you'll be presenting is not groundbreaking. You're not going to get noticed by the Nobel Committee. In fact, we don't want you to get noticed. We don't want you to be a Steven Hawking. We want you to be forgettable," she coaxed.

"Richard, I know you are used to being the pointy end of the spear. Now we need you to be invisible. We need you to blend in so much that no one will remember you," Ms. Jones says sweetly.

"Ms. Jones, as long as we're going to be working together, don't you think it's time I knew your real name? I mean, you know everything about me, and I know absolutely nothing about you," Richard changed the tone of the conversation, friendly, inviting, relaxed.

"For the purposes of this operation, you can call me Catherine, Catherine Ang," she replied. "My late father was a wealthy Chinese immigrant from Hong Kong, who emigrated to the United States. He loved his new adopted home. I now run the architecture and engineering firm he founded. The firm consults with government agencies in Washington DC and around the world," she continued.

"I have a Bachelor's degree from UC Berkeley in California. Like my father, I majored in architecture. The agency recruited me right out of college. I did one or two contract jobs for them and then joined them full time as a direct employee.

We have a lot of work to do, Richard. So you just keep studying and working on your background cover. There can be no mistakes once we're out in the field."

**The End**

Look for *Richard Diamond, CIA* coming soon.

Edward F. Koehler, Ph D lives in Ocean City, Maryland and enjoys sailing on the Chesapeake, playing tennis, and going downhill skiing. He can be contacted at Edward.koehler@aol.com or at www.richardleiter.net.

CPSIA information can be obtained
at www.ICGtesting.com
Printed in the USA
BVHW030251070721
610933BV00001B/2